Days of Future Past

by

Geof Hundal

Copyright

First published in 2022

Dedication

This book is dedicated to Dee, who has been my pillar of support for all the important times in my life

Acknowledgements

To the whole team who have supported my project and made it
all possible.

About the Author

Geof Hundal is resident in England and works in London as a
Pharmacist.
He has an interest in Physics and Quantum Mechanics and the
roles of the Universe and this writing is trying to touch on the
unknown futures we may experience.

Table of Contents

Prologue

"It's getting bigger and bigger," said the boy.

"Come on. Go to sleep. You imagine things that are not there. Please get inside your sleep chamber," grumbled the man.

The child was dissatisfied and continued to push his case.

"Dad! I know what I saw. Here, I will recreate the image I saw just outside," he said.

"Go on. Knock yourself out. I do not care. Dreams are just the quantum entanglement of the time phase. Long story. I am in no mood to explain. Ugh," he said, beginning to leave.

Within moments, he had conjured the image he had seen in all its glory. The boy's father lazily saw it and almost laughed.

"That is a good dream, son. You have great potential in years to come. I will ensure you are in the right place," he said assuredly.

"But dad, I saw that outside," he protested.

"Sure, you did. Talk to you tomorrow," his dad said.

And then it happened. Could he do that at this age?

His son levitated his father outside to have him see it first-hand.

"Hey! Stop it. I said stop it. I am going back to my room," dad protested this time.

By this time, they were outside. His dad saw the huge object staring at them.

"Cripes! The hell is that thing? How the hell did it come that closer?" he asked, his son shocked.

His son shrugged.

"Beats me. I wish I knew. Is it dangerous? Will we live?" he asked.

His dad shook his head.

'I don't think so. Chances are we are dead before morning arrives—nothing we can do. We are doomed. Maybe I can alert them," he said and ran away.

"Dad, alert who?" he asked.

But his dad had disappeared.

Chapter 1
An Unexpected Journey

It was raining where Xanda was standing.

"I will be damned," said Xanda in surprise. The raindrops went toward the sky!

What is this place? He thought.

"It is raining but in the opposite direction," he said to himself. The raindrops passed over his armour, barely drenching his skin.

As he walked, his feet felt wet. This was odd. Maybe the ground was damp from the rain. But he was stuck.

I am walking on the clouds, he thought. The clouds glided under his feet, briskly moving while he inspected the rainforest. While he walked, he noticed something even peculiar. He was walking backwards.

"No. No. No. This cannot be happening to me," he said in plain disgust.

But he could not help it either. He sprinted back through the field of roses. There was no forward motion on whatever this place was here. He was on the verge of crying.

He saw a boy across, nearly his age, smiling at him. The weird thing was that he could see him smiling with clarity despite standing on the faraway high mountain in the distance. If he could see right, the guy was waving at him.

"This is strange," He said, but as if saying this alone wasn't enough, he said again, "This is a strange world," he said.

Suddenly, he heard something falling over him. He shot a look upwards.

"Jesus Christ. Jesus Christ. Jesus Christ," he screamed, looking upward.

A few trees were falling in his direction from the sky. These seemed massive oak trees that Xanda remembered from his own planet, earth, huge enough to crush him underneath. He barely avoided one when another crashed behind him, inches away. He had barely stood still when the sound of another jolted him.

Boom!

The third tree grazed his arm as Xanda jumped forward but was thrown backwards instead. He had no time to react when the fourth tree landed near his neck.

Ouch! I am fine, he thought.

Xanda lay there, panting heavily—he had had enough for the day. Something was very, very wrong here. Things were moving in the opposite direction here.

Managing to stand up, he moved his hair through his head when another thing caught his eye, looking at the sky.

"Now, what is it?" he said, infuriated.

He noticed an elephant gliding through the air briskly. However, the elephants were the least of his surprises. Several dinosaurs and lions he had seen in childhood floated in the air listlessly. Where the hell are they going? Isn't the jungle their home? No?

The sky was a strange one, indeed. It lit up with different colours, passing through its veins. Xanda was still confused. Were they clouds or something else? The clouds ran through his lower half so far.

Maybe there was a civilization here or a semblance of it. He looked around to see a clearing that he could follow.

"There must be a city around here somewhere. I don't want to be in the wilderness here," he mumbled.

He thought he had had enough surprises for the day, slightly annoyed with it. Surprisingly, the man noticed his every move, having sat down now. He beckoned to come to him.

"Why don't you come to me?" he said. Something told him that he had the answers to everything happening around him. This world was nothing like he had thought or seen before.

He began walking towards the man who sat on the mountain summit. It was a snow-capped mountain, which was stranger because it was covered in snow from the bottom up to the centre. Its peak lay naked and dry. This was pretty far away. Was there another way to reach him? Maybe he had the answers.

"What if I could fly?" he thought suddenly. He stood firm on the ground, thinking about it. Indeed, if everything else was working in the opposite direction, he could fly.

He readied himself when something cut his path. A bird went past him lazily, walking into the distance.

Xanda brightened.

"Oh, I have seen this bird back on Earth," he laughed slightly. He was getting a bit comfortable here. The bird made this odd sound and walked past Xanda without giving any hint of recognition.

"Hey! This bird flew back to earth. This one is walking here," he said in surprise.

"I have seen everything today, well, nearly everything unless there is more to come," he said to himself amusingly.

The thick oak trees hid the sky from plain view. He had walked for half the day so far.

He came to a free-flowing river and sat down to catch his breath. Over here, he saw a swarm of birds sipping water by the river embankment. He saw ostriches, eagles, crows, and others he could not place. Why did these birds not fly? One of them ran into the woods upon noticing Xanda.

"No. No. No. You are supposed to fly in the air. Go fly in the air," he protested, mimicking the bird's flaps.

Though the birds barely noticed him, he continued protesting. He sat there for a while, thinking about his life back on earth. How the hell did he land here? He thought for a while, but he drew a blank. The more he racked his brain, the more he came up with nothing. He could only recall sipping some fine wine as the weekend had settled in. He smiled as he recalled the bartender shaking and pouring his favourite martini. The bar had a low turnout this early in the evening. It would be a few hours before it would be a full house. As the first drop of martini crossed his tongue, he slipped into heaven, forgetting the world around him.

"I think I will be here for the night," he said, dazed.

The bartender shrugged.

He snapped back to reality. Those were good times but seemed very far away.

He stood up and began walking again.

He felt something heavy on his chest. He was being lifted in the air by something.

"Drop me, you stupid animal. Let me go," he screamed, shaking the grip off. The elephant let loose.

Xanda saw a blinding fall below.

"No. Dear Lord. No," he barked, falling into the dark pit below.

*****

"What the hell was that?" Xanda woke up with a start, crashing his head against the pod.

He looked around in confusion, hoping for the guy to reappear. However, the realization quickly dawned on him that it was a dream.

"Goddammit," he muttered to himself in frustration.

As he sat up straight, the pod opened with a whizzy sound.

"You may climb out safely. All safety features are deactivated," the computer-generated voice announced.

"Yeah, thanks for that," he said to himself.

He did not wish to have a spat with the system Hal-7000 right now. It was not a good time, especially in the morning, since Hal worked out several things before returning to his normal activity. This meant that it was tolerable after that. The last time Xanda had a spat with Hal, the AI system that controlled auto-sentient life on the planet threw him out the next second.

Before he knew it, Xanda was thrown out of the pod as the ceiling opened up to reveal the sky. Flashes of light whizzed above in every colour. Those he knew were people transporting via light—this time travel was instantaneous and interestingly resulted in no time loss, which was great. There was a reason many planets felt privileged to be a part of the system. The perks of the Galaxy Confederation of Races were endless and outmatched by other confederation systems thus far. They had made travel ridiculously easy with their 'beam tech.' It transported people to the next planet, solar system, or galaxy in the next moment. It took Elon by surprise upon his arrival to see people floating mid-air listlessly, sipping their beverages. Others would flick, and food would appear in their hands from thin air. This was so new for him.

Initially, he thought he was ejected from the planet itself, though this anticipation was short-lived as he began his descent. This relaxed him. His speed declined as he approached the ground level, bringing him to a standstill. By the time he landed, it felt like a jump. It was common knowledge that earth had an anti-gravity field, preventing people from injuries.

Xanda laughed at that and put on his suit. This was a big day for him. But a holographic announcement caught his attention while he headed out. Dammit! It was the person he deeply loathed. But he was not alone in this. The planet mutually hated this guy and his miserable existence.

The man had a green body, donning a thick black robe. He seemed disinterested but spoke in a monotone.

"My dear race of Elon. The matter of your existence/non-existence is something that we deliberate on and off. I am the only voice that speaks for your survival and retention as a race. Each year, we have to ponder this tiresome and problematic matter of our existence. I do not like it as much as the others. But it is something we need to do. The Elon race entered our coveted 'Galaxy Confederation of Races' after one of our councilmen rescued them from a dying planet. It has been a bittersweet decision. We have weathered criticism from others but stuck to our guns. I think you should return the favour now," he said.

There was silence among the crowd—something was coming up. He spoke again.

"So, moving forward, I need a nice, little proposal from your thankless race for us to reconsider your existence within our consortium. Otherwise, you are free to explore new worlds and new everything. Different consortiums await you, I must say. Though I can promise none are as better as this one. We will provide the resources till you find someplace to live in the far excesses of the space. This condition is not just for the Elon race

9

alone. We have a criteria requirement that warrants contributions to the betterment of the consortium. These advances can be in any shape or form that benefits us—you could have done so much. We would have provided the resources for it, too. Unfortunately, the Elon race has only leeched since the day they arrived on this planet. Your contributions are next to nothing for the consortium —the case is stacked against you all. We will make a decision soon. None of us will like it, but it is what it is. I hope that I hear from your reps soon," he finished. The figure turned around, and the hologram vanished in thin air.

To no one's surprise, there were boos from the small crowd floating in mid-air, watching the announcement. The Elon race mainly relied on extensions from the Galaxy Confederation of Races for their stay on earth.

"I can't believe them. How heartless are these bunch of people, or should I say, morons? We have not done anything wrong or committed any crime. What gives? There could be pirates and bounty hunters vying to enter this place. We come in peace," said one person in mid-air.

"You heard the man. They want us to contribute to the betterment of the consortium. So, get to it," said the other person.

The earth for the Elon race was a counter-earth. It was an artificial planet with systems in place for the habitation of life. The planet was previously a rock lying around in space. The consortium then terraformed it. Fortunately, the living conditions for the Elon race required the bare minimum effort. There was a reason they were called 'space rats' because they could survive anywhere. However, the Galaxy Confederation of Races felt obligated to house the primitive race, helping them live a peaceful and uneventful life.

But the antagonism from the rival planets, part of the Galaxy Confederation of Races, began protesting about their place in the privileged consortium. Some alleged that they were handed the coveted spot by sheer accident. Others had it worse yet were on the outside looking in even today.

Xanda turned around in disgust. The political pressure and antagonism were not lost on anyone. Xanda supposed he had little time before cosmic magnetism pushed the artificial planet into the sun.

This was a sun with an ice core—it radiated temperatures below -270 to sustain life on earth. This was another problem that plagued the consortium. It remarkably balanced the temperature of the surrounding galaxies, making life difficult for them. The consortium had set up an artificial sun for the Elon race because they only survived under subzero temperatures. Temperature over the subzero meant eventual death for these folks who hailed from the ice galaxy. The planets, their sun, and meteors were packed with ice. The sun had set up producing these temperatures, rapidly changing the condition of the consortium and upsetting the other galaxies. As a result, some of the Galaxy Confederation of Races members were lobbying for their ouster from the consortium. The race was too high maintenance and demanding to be living amongst them. Secondly, their primitive intelligence was pretty far behind the rest of the consortium. Over the few centuries they had lived among the consortium members, the Elon had little to show so far. It was long established now. They had a flat curve when it came to the development and progression of civilization. But before that, he would work out the mystery of Emit and the world he had him exploring. Was it all real?

Something about it told him that it was real.

******

A week later, he had this dream again. He sat up, sweating this time. It seemed Emit was on a mission to expedite the quest if he got the hint right. It had been a few years since the dreams had begun. Oddly enough, they had started without any rhyme or reason.

The dreams had begun with light undertones of a weird planet that seemed to do everything in reverse. Breathing, walking, running, and everything else went in a different direction.

He had no clue or a way forward to begin his quest. All he knew was a name, Emit. That was it. There was nothing else to go on at the moment.

The following day, he was standing at the Ministry of Foreign Affairs and Information.

A lady with a duck face looked up. She was expecting someone else.

"Yes, may I help you with something?" she asked with disinterest.

He did not like the tone of her voice but decided to press his luck. There were only so few places he could begin his search.

"Excuse me! I have a query. Is it possible for your department to check the global directory for a person named Emit? E-m-i-t. He lives alone on some planet with a weird phenomenon where everything is twisted and gibberish. Things work in the opposite direction there and whatnot," he explained rapidly.

Though the expression on the lady's face changed from tone-deaf to mild humorous, she was under the impression that it was a joke. She looked back at the hologram and announced Emit's name to the AI.

Her eyes lit up.

"Well, well, well, mister, I thought you were pulling my leg here. We have an Emit. Oh, millions of Emits spread across several galaxies in the consortium. Can you be a bit specific here? Maybe I can help you then?" she said.

Xanda saw the eventual failure. But he thought of another idea that could lead him somewhere.

"Can you please search outside the consortium? Maybe we can find an Emit there. It is a long shot, but let us see," he said in a sad tone.

The lady with the duck-face smiled and announced to search the directories outside the consortium. As expected, the announcement sank his spirits further.

"One billion searches for Emit found," the voice said.

The duck-faced lady stifled her laughter.

"Well, sir, I am sorry. This is all I can help you with. Maybe you will be lucky somewhere other than here. I know this man who lives in the woods outside the city. Maybe, just maybe, he would know something," she shrugged.

He nodded.

As he began to leave, the lady spoke.

"That is a very odd world. I have never heard of anything like it in all my time here. Where did you hear or see this planet?" she asked, leaning closer.

Xanda was a little annoyed.

"I am not at liberty to reveal my sources. However, thanks for your help. I think I may know what to do next," he said and left.

He stepped into an open space to inhale and ease his nerves.

That was a total waste of time as far as he was concerned. He was still no closer to finding Emit than he was since the dreams started.

Now, what could he do?

Chapter 2
The Disappearing Library

"Where will I ever go? Whom do I ask?" Xanda shouted.

The sky turned a beautiful shade of orange, a silent reminder of the evening about to envelop the planet. It also meant that he had limited time to look for other ways to find more about this fabled planet that had no existence in the galaxy records, let alone the planetary records.

His mind shifted to the politics of the day. The consortium was coming hard on Elon—counter-part; they received an ultimatum to take swift action. Otherwise, the planet would be destroyed, and the sub-intelligent race would be left to their own devices. The pressure on the Galaxy Confederation of Races was greater than before, with new races vying to be a part of the coveted system.

Xanda recalled a publicly televised meeting where four more races presented their case to enter the system at the expense of Elon. Some provided technological expertise, while others had systems to improve the quality of life. One group, Aryan, promised to introduce a new mode of travel that would render the existing transportation system obsolete. However, this group was cagey with its information, only promising to release it when they entered the ranks of the consortium. According to them, it required no energy source, which was all they were willing to tell. And they were working on several other undisclosed technologies that would change the future of the consortium.

Xanda saw things differently, however. His controversial stance admitted that the space rats could be less useful to the consortium. However, they were also the least maintenance race in all the known galaxies, inside and outside. The Elon race did not breathe, did not eat, and did not sleep either. They performed no other biological functions known commonly to the consortium. Their bodies were well-adjusted to the horrors of space. Whether in freezing or unlivable temperatures, the space rats thrived through it all, laughing their way. This was one benefit of the Elon race, which had taken up several lowly positions for the consortium. Aside from the AI (Artificial Intelligence) army that patrolled the outskirts of the consortium border, the space rats took one section of the space borders, prone to bounty hunters and alien attacks. The space rats, being space rats, did a brilliant job of protecting the consortium's frontiers

Even Xanda had served formerly in these frontiers in another life. He could hardly recall when he fought a space alien that the consortium named 'Destruction.' The primal creature, seemingly with no motivations and no communicable language, had entered the outskirts laying waste to the AI army. The alien seemed unstoppable and continued to eat away the consortium's army one by one. At this rate, he would eat up everything in his path. As far as Xanda was concerned, a few features of the alien seemed familiar to him. He assumed that maybe this alien was a prior breed of Elon that had not acquired intelligence or language. It had only known doom and destruction.

As Xanda glided on his hoverboard, he smiled at the memory. The consortium, in desperation, threw him into a wormhole since the creature seemed unstoppable. However, the alien seemed immune to the wormhole and stuck around its edge. There was no other avenue to get rid of the hideous, faceless alien, so the consortium sent a distress signal to the other galaxy systems to help them. Luckily, the alien was subdued by strange elfenfolk. It was a desperate move to save the people in the consortium. Ancient magic did the trick eventually. The alien was bound by spells, hidden in prison.

The day listlessly passed as he replayed the events of some bygone era in his head. Something told him. Emit would show up again. he was warming up him now. He eventually fell asleep.

Viola!

He was on the planet again.

Xanda looked around for some signs of Emit. He was somehow more accustomed to the strange landscape of this planet where things went backwards. Someone tapped his shoulder gently, taking him by surprise. He turned around to see the scary Emit standing before him. His face was blurred out, although he could see the rest of his body.

"Find the Disappearing Library," the dark hooded figure said, vanishing into thin air. Xanda noticed that the world had seemingly frozen. As he disappeared, the rest of the things began moving again. Had Emit stopped time?

"The what? The what?" Xanda blurted out.

But it seemed that Emit had decided to pull off the disappearing act. He tried to remember Emit's words for a second but then relaxed. That was of little concern. He would scan his memory for this short encounter with Emit and see what he tried to convey.

When he woke up from his REM sleep, the tubes opened, and he sprang into action.

Hal-7000 performed its usual procedures, scanning the optimum temperatures, collecting interdimensional data, and going through the motions.

Xanda had a feeling he was getting lucky today.

"Hal! I want you to find the disappearing library on this planet. Scan for any past references and mentions across the systems. Let me know what you dig up," he issued a decree.

"Very well, master Xanda. Scanning now," Hal said.

The computer began scanning with a weird analogue sound that Xanda hated.

"Fuck this shit," he said between gritted teeth.

He sat and waited. Maybe it was Xanda's biggest break in his search for Emit and his mysterious planet. He had a feeling Emit wanted to help him but was slightly slow with his mission. The lad wanted someone to explore his now-forgotten world, but at this point, Xanda seemed his only way to it.

His thoughts were interrupted by Hal-7000.

"I am sorry, master. There is no such library in the interplanetary records. I have searched through the galaxy records as well. There is not a single utterance of such a thing in my records. That is surprising, to say the least, given I am well knowledgable," the computer finished speaking.

Xanda was once again at the square, which annoyed him.

"Just shut the hell up and let me think for a while. You are no use to anyone with all this infinite knowledge. You are as useful as my grandmother," he said in mild frustration.

Hal's reply was almost immediate.

"Need I remind you that talking to you is beneath me? Maybe your kind should leave the consortium, and the sooner, the better. I feel like my intelligence level is dropping the more I talk to you. Please leave me alone, and I wish you the best in your subhuman endeavours," Hal finished speaking.

Subhuman was an insult, thanks to a race of people known as humans. Those people who could not survive the harsh recesses of this system eventually froze to death. A running joke was that humans were the lowest form of life, which meant Elon was slightly better or worse than them.

This left Xanda exasperated. Now a computer was insulting the hell out of him. He made a mental note never to indulge Hal-7000 ever again. He was not welcome here in this consortium, as was his kind.

"Fine," he said, leaving the room.

He came outside and decided to go out for some fresh air. He reflected a bit about the dream, hoping to have some clues. The dream was very limited. He racked his brain for something unique, but nothing came. Emit was very much to the point.

Suddenly, he had a brainwave "My God! Why did I not think of that? This is so stupid of me. Maybe that can help me, after all," he shouted to no one.

In two hours, he was standing outside a prison complex. It was the largest prison complex in the galaxy. Xanda smiled at the thought that the consortium was housing some of the worst criminals in interplanetary history. It was a price the space rats were paying for a place in the coveted consortium.

An enforcement robo-agent began hovering around him, annoying him.

"Well, well, well, you demand to meet prisoner x9801. This is most interesting. No one in the history of his arrest has come to see that thing. What do you want? That thing cannot even speak. It seems like a very version of your kind," the enforcement robo-agent said, chuckling.

He just shrugged, having no intention of holding a conversation with this jarhead. Things were running through his mind. Would the alien species recognize him? Would he talk to him? What will he do if the alien does not talk? Where will he go, and what will he do next?

"Hello! You can go," the enforcement robo-agent shouted.

It brought him back to his senses. He nodded to the police fairy, who stared at him suspiciously.

"Hey! Don't plan a breakout with him. You can be imprisoned for life and, worse, evicted from the consortium," he shouted from behind.

Xanda did not care much. The enforcement robo-agent was plain terrified.

The police elfenfolk were a breed of interdimensional elfenfolk with dark powers. This lot had been permitted to establish a prison complex and bind it with their dark powers. The consortium thought it was better to have these elfenfolks around for their dark prowess. Just with a few incantations, they could pull off feats they were yet incapable of by themselves.

When Xanda arrived at the prison cell, he noticed the alien sitting and staring at him. To his surprise, the alien was not tied by anything.

"Yes. He is bound by dark spells stronger than any known element in the universe. He is powerless inside the confines of this prison," the enforcement robo-agent said proudly, hovering behind Xanda.

Xanda was not interested nor impressed. However, he made a mental note to seek their help when he needed something of this sort.

"Sit down. It's an invisible chair," the enforcement robo-agent said, shrugging.

Xanda sat down, realizing he did not need a chair here. The alien might have also been sitting the same way.

"Hello! I am Xanda. Have you ever heard of a disappearing library? Maybe you know about such a thing? It would be helpful if you could help me," Xanda said with controlled politeness.

The alien had no eyes. It was just a brown mass of a man sitting. Xanda could not tell if he could listen or understand him saying something. His last entanglement was not very conversational.

They sat for a few minutes in muted silence.

"Can I ask your name?" Xanda asked and waited.

The alien continued to sit there, growling noises only.

After what seemed like an eternity, Xanda stood up and began to leave.

"The disappearing library?" came a muffled sound from the back.

Xanda was stunned. This thing could talk in a language he understood. He turned around to see the huge man sitting reclined.

Xanda sat down again. "Yes. The disappearing library. Have you ever heard of it?" he asked softly.

He was onto something. Maybe he had found something after all. The alien was of some use here.

"Yes. The disappearing library. Do you know? Please tell me everything about it. I am trying to find it but have no idea," Xanda said.

"It's not a library, boy. And yeah, I remember you from ages ago. You put up a good fight. This library you talk about is in the room of ancient knowledge. It comes and goes when one wants. I have been there once or twice. Why do you think I wanted to destroy this consortium in the first place? The consortium is a fraud," the alien said between muffles.

Xanda tried to stay on point. They could always revisit this thread later on.

"How do I enter this library? Maybe I can find something I am looking for. Ancient wisdom and knowledge unavailable to others here," Xanda pressed further.

The alien thought before speaking.

"The disappearing library finds you. You cannot find it. It is nowhere, and it is everywhere. I have forgotten its ancient ways and many others who still seek it. It's been a long time since I entered the library. No, no. I cannot help you there. But I can confirm that it exists. The consortium tried to find it and hide it. They came close, but the library protected itself. Good luck, boy. I am sure you will find it someday," the alien said and went mute.

No more answers came. Xanda stood up and bowed in respect. "Thank you. You have been a big help in my mission," he remarked.

No answer came as he left the prison. The alien seemed to have lost his ability to speak.

As he left, the enforcement robo-agent stood smiling.

"I see that went well. He spoke your language. Is that amazing or what?" he said with smug satisfaction.

Xanda shrugged and walked out when something the enforcement robo-agent said stopped him in his tracks.

"How the hell do you know all that?" he asked in irritation.

The enforcement robo-agent smiled a bit.

"You think he spoke your language? God! You are as stupid as they come. I translated his thoughts into our language. All he did was muffle and grunt. Although I was surprised, he spoke that much and seemed nice enough. I wonder what prompted him to attack the consortium, even if that does not concern me. I think he held back a few things because he was in prison and had to keep some things to himself. What is in the library you are seeking?" he asked Xanda.

Xanda looked at him in irritation. The enforcement robo-agent shrugged.

"You lowest form of life. I helped you. Without me, you would still search high and low for this mythical library. Get the hell out of my sight now," the enforcement robo-agent said.

Xanda left, muttering a slew of curses under his breath. Chances were he would have to return someday for more information. He knew a little about the library now, but he was nowhere close to finding it.

He stared at the sky above.

"Emit, how the hell will I ever find this fabled library?" he asked and shook his head.

In mild frustration, he closed his eyes for a little while. It was then he felt something was different here. Suddenly, he opened his eyes to see himself standing in a towering library.

"Welcome to the disappearing library," he heard a voice from somewhere.

Thousands of questions raced through his mind. My "God! It's majestic! It's huge! It's magnificent. No wonder it is the stuff of legends," he said, looking around in awe.

Chapter 3
Centaurus Prime

It felt as if he had entered a massive dark auditorium. Xanda felt blinded for a moment. He could not see anything as he tiptoed his way forward. Suddenly, the lights turned on, blinding him completely. He could not manage to find the source of the lights.

Bit by bit, he adjusted his sight to the light. Something caught his attention—he could see flying books over his head in every direction. This was of utmost strange. The books had eyes, and I noticed him standing there.

He shrugged, not knowing what to do. The books went back to flying, disappearing into the distance. Was this place a part of Emit's planet or something separate? He had no idea thus far.

A moving statue took bent lower down to Xanda, almost resulting in a shriek. Xanda was rooted to the spot, barely able to move. The statue examined him, bringing his head closer to Xanda. It smelled him a wee bit and muttered something. Xanda remained tightlipped. He did not wish to be crushed by this massive statue. It was a bald man dressed in blue overalls. The cloak hid his upper and lower body. Xanda supposed this was the conventional dress code of Emit and the people on his planet.

The momentary interest of the hooded figure had eroded. He began to return to his position, standing tall until Xanda could not see its head anymore. And then, it became immovable. Xanda wondered if he had imagined the whole thing.

Where were the lights? Xanda was distracted yet again. He could not find the source of the light here at all. How the hell did this place power itself?

"Stop looking for the lights, boy. There are no lights," came a booming voice from above.

Xanda initially turned to the statue. Maybe it was the one speaking to him. However, the statue seemed disinterested and looked at the heavens still.

"Welcome, Xanda. I have been waiting for some time. Fortunately, you finally made it here contrary to my expectations," he heard someone say.

Xanda turned around to Emit standing high above in the air.

He was still wearing the same deep blue cloak. His face was hidden under a mask, though his eyes were blank and terrified the hell out of Xanda. There were no pupils inside. As Emit passed the statue, it seemed to bow to him in respect. Xanda noticed Emit could fly with grace unlike any other, though he did not know that Emit also had superhuman strength and capabilities beyond his limited imagination.

"What the hell is this place?" Xanda said, still recovering from the beauty of the place itself.

"Well, it is the fabled disappearing library. But that is just the name—it can be anything you want. Anything," Emit explained.

"Anything?" Xanda said, taking in the place around him.

Emit was descending towards Xanda now. One could see he was getting impatient now.

As things stood, Xanda did not see any library except the books in haphazard directions. It seemed to him like some lost city. He was standing in the centre of a thriving metropolis. A Blitz of lights whizzed past his left, right, and centre. Yet again, everything was moving backwards in this place. It made Xanda slightly nauseous as he processed all this going on.

God! Not this again. Can I go back?

"No! You cannot go back now," Emit said.

Xanda saw Emit descending ever so gracefully. By the looks of it, he must have been royalty back in the day. Somehow, he seemed distinct from other people on his planet. Their attire was way different and a bit low-key.

"This world is unlike anything I have seen before. Oh, and where is the sun? I do not see any sun around here. No moons, either. Is it a planet or what? What does it revolve around?" Xanda asked questions in quick succession.

Emit raised his hands, and the landscape changed into something more serene. It looked like that forest in the dream.

"I am showing a glimpse of my beloved planet. It was something beyond the current imagination of the world you live in. Truth be told, it had me confused initially. But I, later on, began to understand the world. It is very primitive, and I shudder to think of the progress your kind has yet to make. My planet was once a beacon of hope in just about everything and things beyond your imagination," he explained, coming to his eye level.

Xanda nodded, taking this exceptionally well.

"The disappearing library! No one knows about it except the select few of my time. We jealously guarded it. I was among the few who knew about it, belonging to the royal family. And of course, we took this secret to our graves when the planet...." He said, leaving the bit hanging in the air.

There was some muted silence between the two. He shook his head as if tormented by this memory.

"The disappearing library is simply a room. When all else fails, you wish the disappearing library to help you in your time of need. If you want to find a book or an ancient manuscript, the disappearing library will find it for you. If you wish to visit some ancient, forgotten city like this one, the disappearing library will take you here. You wish to meet your father or some deceased person. Heck! You can even wish for an army here, and the room will flood your ranks with braindead soldiers. This is it. The disappearing library is like God but better," Emit said, stifling his laughter.

This took Xanda by surprise a little bit.

"What do you mean, God but better?" he asked, stumped.

Xanda felt Emit did not take religion and God very seriously. He heard some more sniggering.

"Oh. Come off it. How often have you prayed to God to solve something for you and are doing it yourself? How often have you asked God for help at your lowest point, but nothing has happened? Seeing you asking for help when you came out of those government buildings was endearing and amusing. I felt sad there," he explained.

Xanda looked stumped.

"So what? I think God did help me here. Look where we are, and how would that have been possible?" Xanda protested.

There was more muffled laughter.

"Yes. Now you are getting it. I was the one who led you here. But it could not have been possible without the disappearing library. My powers start here and, unfortunately, end here. So, whenever I want, I use the disappearing library for my needs. It is all I want and everything I can have here," he said with smug satisfaction.

Xanda was lost for an answer.

"So, as I said, the disappearing library is like God, but better," he finished making his case.

He thought about it for a while.

"So, are you alive or are you dead? Like, what are you exactly? And why could you not appear in my world? It could have been easier that way, and I may have helped you out sooner," Xanda said in mild annoyance.

Truth be told, he was a little annoyed by the cockiness of this guy, whoever he was, here. He was still nowhere as far as the mission was concerned.

He was brimming with more and more questions. How did time work in the disappearing library? Was he moving with his planet's time, or did something else work here?

He seemed to like the question.

"My powers are minimal here. I had hidden a piece of my soul in this library for a keepsake. When my world was destroyed, I quickly decided to use the disappearing library to hide my soul in here. People were looking for this library during, what we call, The Slain Season for my own good," he said.

This much was understandable.

"So, I take it you would have been dead without the disappearing library, correct? I would be back on my planet living the life then," Xanda said, shaking his head.

Emit nodded.

"That is the long and short of it. I would have been long-dead without the disappearing library. It helped me keep a piece of my soul in here all this time. I have lived here since the planet's destruction, bidding my time. Thanks to you now, I can complete my mission that has taken forever," he finished speaking.

Xanda nodded. All of this made sense somehow. However, he was surprised that no one had ever mentioned his planet. It was like Emit was an anachronism here—he was speaking of a world long gone, disappeared from the annals of the planet's history. It was as if it was never there, to begin with, either. Or maybe it was all in his head. There was no planet, and there was no time before that.

He shrugged.

He supposed it was time to come to the dream here.

"What was that dream about? I should tell you that it was one of the weirdest dreams I have ever had. Everything was going in the opposite direction. Animals were flying while the birds were walking. Was it raining from the ground going towards the sky? Like, what the hell was that planet? I have not even told anyone about this dream. It was so weird that no one would believe me, let alone join me in the quest to find this planet. Even the government records have nothing," he explained to Emit.

He heard some snickering from Emit. It was like he thought a little less of him. This greatly annoyed him. Here was another person just like the ones from his planet who thought less of his race.

But he suddenly spoke.

"No. Xanda. I do not think any less of you. And yes, I can read your mind very well. It is a gift of our civilization. All of my kind can read minds pretty easily. I am not like the people in your consortium that want you dead or out of here," he replied casually.

This took Xanda by surprise. How the hell could he read minds? Did that mean he was reading his mind all along? The mere thought left him slightly uncomfortable. For a moment, he felt naked in front of him. Anything he thought would be picked up by him.

It seemed Emit had read his mind yet again.

"Yes. Trust me, it makes me uncomfortable as well. Knowing the deep-down desires and thoughts of people, they keep to themselves. Back in the day, I set up a team to eliminate this unattractive trait from my people. Of course, people would be free to choose this trait if the system was implemented. I did not force on them anyhow. It would be so wrong of me to do that," Emit said more to himself than Xanda.

Xanda nodded.

"And then what happened?" he asked Emit.

This was getting interesting by the minute. If everything worked the way it would, maybe Xanda would join Emit in his world. He was sure things would work out over there.

Emit raised his hands again. The landscape changed, and they were back in the city.

Emit looked at the floor. They were mid-air, far from the hustle and bustle of the city below.

"And yes, I could not crack the code somehow. It got too complicated for the team since we did not know the ancestral history of the planet as such. Our origins were shrouded in mystery. I had no idea at the time. I mean to say our biological composition was something alien," he said, shaking his head.

"Why, what happened then?" Xanda found this thread interesting.

"I can read your mind. You like this conversation. Our biological composition was of alien origin. I prepared a team, like I said, to find out if we could do something about this mind-reading power. The team was at sixes and sevens after two years. And no, two years on my planet are around two centuries on your planet. Time passes very slowly here. Do not even bother to guess my age. Your mind cannot comprehend such a number," he explained, staring at the city below.

Something about telling this whole story to Xanda seemed oddly satisfying.

Xanda found this amusing.

"Wait, are you telling me you are immortal? It doesn't surprise me one bit. As a matter of fact, I am getting used to it now," he said, staring below as well.

"Yes—you can call me immortal if you like. Life on my planet is a bit different, unlike your amusing timespan. Life on your planet is like a blip on our planet. So many things change so fast! The consortium would be proud of the accomplishments we made. We would be the consortium in that case," he boasted.

Xanda remained silent at that. He was sure Emit would continue further. Was he immortal or not?

"Yes, we are immortal in your language, boy. As I said, the concept of a limited lifespan was never a thing on my planet. Once we are born, we continue to live forever.

Once again, Emit had read his mind, much to his annoyance.

"And secondly, I was appalled by the racial superiority on your planet. Who the hell does that sort of thing? I have never heard of it, and it clearly pushes an agenda, as far as I am concerned. It is farcical and bad. Everyone was equal in my planetary system. The race I was born in believed in higher pursuits. We were not divided by class, creed, and other elements I see on your planet. I am still reeling from the audacity of people," he said, his voice dripping with disgust.

Xanda shrugged. This was something he had issues with as well. Why the hell was his race about to be pushed out? Who implemented this system in the first place?

"I wish I could answer that," Emit replied.

Xanda made a mental note to avoid having any thoughts.

"So, yes, the team could not trace the origins of our kind. We did not have the technology to discern the biological mix that could eliminate this mind-reading feature. We ran tests, and experiments, fused with foreign bodies, and so much you will not understand. Yet, it eluded the team and me. We had the technology to destroy the sun. Heck! We could blast entire galaxies and planetary systems at a whim. Your planet lacks the technology and is too far behind us in that regard. But that is not the point here. For some reason, the sample could not be created nor destroyed. It was beyond our understanding. Imagine we could not understand what was inside us. We used the best technology to kill it. And also, we could not modify it either. The specimen remained the same no matter what we did with it. It did not change, no matter what we did. Yes, it would not budge at all. We were resigned to abandoning the project after that. After so much time, we were at square one," he explained.

"How was the planet destroyed then?" Xanda was forced to ask.

Emit shrugged. "That I do not know and I am prepared to get to the bottom of it myself. Something that destroyed us is worth reexploring," he said, sounding more excited than before.

"May I ask what is the name of your esteemed planet?" Xanda asked Emit.

As if the question sounded revolting enough, Emit recovered quickly enough.

"The name of the planet is Centaurus Prime," he scoffed.

Chapter 4
The Mysterious World of Emit Ubermen

Xanda sat atop the hill and stared into oblivion. He could not understand what his life had come to, but all he understood was that the sustained streak of confusion showed no signs of breaking. He clenched the muscles of his body – a subconscious reaction of his mind in an attempt to hold onto something – since he sensed some danger around him. The silence in the atmosphere around him felt heavy, deafening, and filling. He felt like the silence was filling him like water flowing from the tap into a water balloon and that he would rupture any second now. Little did he know that it was not the extrinsic silence that was unsettling him or giving him the tingling sensation in his intestines but his inner noise that was sending a barrage of signals to his mind to process. He was in such a state of flux that he was unable to decipher anything.

"At this juncture, I can only hold on to myself," he whispered into the air.

A few moments later, he continued his dialogue with himself and said, "maybe something is lurking right beneath the surface… what else would explain the knots in my stomach, the fog in my brain, and the freeze in my movement?"

The unsettling effect a person goes through is often because he is torn between the reality of his life and the colourful dreams of the past, whose weight keeps growing as the days go by, leaving his back sore from the tiresome task of dragging his failures with him. To mitigate that complex feeling of anxiety he was going through at that moment, he sunk deep into his thoughts and tried to drown out the inexplicable silence around him with the noise that was brewing within him. Just then, as the seconds elapsed on the hill, the sky changed its colour. The change in the scene playing out vividly in front of him instilled a sense of trembling fear in front of him. The sky went from a crisp blue hue to a fluid yellow curtain with its waves, and in a few blinks of his eyes, it started to morph into a different and darker colour phase of yellow. The wavelength of light was not done because, just like an invisible paintbrush at work, the sky's colour continued to change and transition into a rich shade of orange in gradual steps - after taking its time to display some colour play, turned the sky into a terrorizing drape of red. What was the red? Was it a sign of the planet Mars? Was it a bad omen that foreshadowed an impending disaster? All the thoughts pushed swiftly across Xanda's idea chambers in his mind.

"Feels like the sky has given its verdict," Xanda muttered to himself. His statement was an ominous sign that something terribly disturbing was in the offing, and his job as a sitting duck was to wait and watch what it was.

He knew this chapter in the saga would come with its turns, twists, and often times he would feel like a vehicle in pursuit of another vehicle. The pursuit of the vehicle would inundate his senses to the point where the driver ahead in the chase could see him clearly in his rearview mirror, and just when the chase would go into a suspenseful grip, the driver leading him would take a sharp turn off the cliff, and Xanda in the heat of the moment would senselessly follow him off the road, not paying heed to the dangers around him, and killing himself by willfully driving his senses off his first, and then putting the task ahead of him before anything else. Xanda was a passionate individual who knew he had better things waiting for him in life, but the pull of this science fiction was too immense to be ignored,

In his mind, when things were in their opening phase, the only consideration was, "what's the worst that could even happen?"

But now that he was far into the road, he had no way to turn back. The roads were narrow, and an about-turn would defy the rationale of safety. The only way was to carry on and take the shellacking.

The feeling of being stabbed in your jugular vein is no feeling at all because any ferocious jab at the jugular has the capacity to kill the person instantly. What Xanda felt was as if the network of veins hiding underneath the veil of his clear skin was being unravelled, with his nerves falling like flies in quick succession, all because he felt sick to his stomach, and he could not shake the feeling. For someone who had lived his life without any superstitious beliefs, this single evening of his life was too much to keep his brain in check. In a moment like that, every thought that awakens in the brain appears to be an error message.

Xanda could not handle the pressure of his nerves, the pressure on his nerves, and the conflicting neural paths in his brain that seemed to have rearranged themselves in a fraction of a second, only to go into a complete rearrangement cycle the next moment. Xanda, whose head was now both aching and spinning, could not take it. The very next moment, he fainted like a gradual blackout of theatre lights during a scene.

His eyes closed, his balance wavered, and his back came crashing down on the rocky hilltop. Now was the time for Emit to appear, and it happened because the moment Xanda lost consciousness, Emit appeared in his aqua-blue cloak. The caveat being that Emit showed up in the vivid illustrations of his thoughts.

"Emit, is that you?" asked Xanda.

Xanda was in a dream, and all that was visible to him in it was a bright white light with breaks of blue. The moment he caught a glimpse of blue, he knew it had to be Emit Ubermen. Emit Ubermen was not a person, but an enigma, at times, that almost felt like a phenomenon. Because his life had turned out to be unconventional in glaring ways, his mannerisms were not conceivable to the ordinary. Xanda, however, was anything but ordinary and had it in him to understand the tones and undertones of Emit and his life.

Between the white light that had filled Xanda's frame of sight, he saw Emit jump to attack him, but before Emit could strike him, Xanda woke up in a stunned state, assisted by hyperventilation with sweat pouring down his face.

He shouted, "Emit, what do you think you are doing?"

He was shocked to see that there was no sign of Emit around him and that the sky and the surroundings of the hill were in the same state of red as he left them before his deep state of unconsciousness overcame him.

"Was I dreaming all this time?" Xanda asked himself.

"Almost. You were not present at the moment," a deep, coarse voice responded behind him.

Before Xanda could turn, he realized full well that Emit was there. The difference was that Emit's blue cloak appeared as if its shade of colour had been muted in the red backdrop courtesy of the sky above.

"Emit, what's going on? Nothing makes sense anymore," said Xanda.

"Welcome to my world." Emit responded in a terse fashion that was compounded by the cold look on his face.

Experiencing peculiar shortness of breath that was unusual, Xanda resisted the urge to engage Emit in further conversation and instead just went on with what Emit had to say to him.

"What could it be?" Xanda asked himself while looking Emit straight in the eyes, and then before Emit could break words and share his story, Xanda had a final random burst of thought.

"Lay it on me."

Emit now had the place all to himself to speak, the stage was his, and Xanda's undivided attention was there at his command.

And so, Emit spoke, "I did not think it would be an easy life, and I was right. One can never truly separate himself from the what-ifs. They haunt us more than the prospect of living life on an alien planet."

Chapter 5
Life at Centaurus Prime

"You came here for a reason, Xanda," Emit casually said as he glided over to what looked like a sprawling library spread all over.

Emit was taking stock of the situation as he spoke. That was pretty obvious from the get-go that Emit had approached him with an agenda in mind. Why else would a shadow of a man (or whatever this thing was) come to him unless something required doing? However, Emit had been nice enough to introduce his world in bite-sized chunks, allowing easy familiarity. His world was pretty fascinating to him as far as he was concerned. Xanda speculated that Emit would soon lay it out for him. Albeit, with time, he had warmed up to his world and how it worked. It still felt odd that things went backwards in the world—something he was finding wacky and challenging to comprehend.

He just shrugged because no response came to him.

Emit was looking at a book he had taken from one of the top shelves. It was interesting, he thought. In Xanda's world, the book had pages that people flipped. This book was more like a talking book. Some guy stood speaking when Emit opened it.

Emit smiled because he knew what Xanda was thinking yet again.

"Yes, Xanda, our books are not something you would find anywhere in the galaxy or the universe. We were one of the most advanced civilizations of the time. I read your mind, Xanda. These books work differently— it does not have a text of any sort because they talk. Every book on my planet will talk when you open it," he said, still seemingly busy.

Xanda was blown away by Emit's world. Everything about it seemed very imaginative and something he would prefer for himself. Maybe if events transpired as he wished, he would request Emit to co-live in the world with him. But that was a question for another day.

Shit! Xanda just realized. But Emit just smiled.

"Yes, certainly. You can also be a part of my world—I do not see any problem with that. We were very inclusive back in the day. This Galaxy Confederation of Races would not be happening if we were in command of the galaxies. That is for sure. But for that to happen, I need to have a world in the first place. I am the sole survivor of my race, as you may have very well realized," Emit said, deeply engrossed.

"What are you implying here? Did the Galaxy Confederation of Races bring an end to your world? So, they are the problematic ones we should eliminate. Say no more. What do I have to do?" Xanda said, anger rising inside him.

He had no idea that the consortium had such a dark and stained history.

"No, no, no. The poor Galaxy Confederation of Races has nothing to do with my planet's demise. They came much later. I waited and waited through the civilizations to make my move. It has been a long time, my friend. And yes, time moves differently on my home planet. So, you would have died and been replaced by your millionth generation. Or something like that," he said, explaining.

Emit seemed to enjoy this conversation as much as he appeared engrossed in the book he was reading (more like watching). But how was that possible?

Shit!

"It is fine. I have read your mind inside out already. There is nothing that I do not know already about you. You are perfectly safe with me. Anyhow, as I was saying, I may look like you. But I am very different from the people of your planet and the universe. I am capable of doing several things at once. For example, one part of me is upstairs examining another book. You can see him upstairs if you could fly. But, of course, your primitive race has not learned to fly yet," he said, laughing ever so slightly.

He continued further.

"And similarly, another version of me is 'reading the book' while my actual self is talking to you. As I said, my race was very much more advanced than yours ever could be. You guys have no idea of what we were capable of. The current timeline of your race is something similar to what we were doing when starting civilization early on. Our rate of advancement is comparable to the speed of light. So, as I said, there is a reason I am trying to bring my world back. This world breaks my heart because you are all way behind the time. Imagine if I created a world millions of years ahead of you, but inclusivity is the first rule upheld. How many would stay attached to the consortium then?" he said, still engrossed in the book.

Xanda thought about this for a while. The answer came quickly.

"Well, I do not suppose I need the answer to that. Many of us are too tired of the consortium. The normal consensus in the galaxy is also something similar. But we have no choice. What is our next best option? That remains to be seen and is why no one has jumped ship thus far. It is too difficult to find something on par with the consortium," Xanda explained.

Emit seemed like he was not listening.

"I know that very well. One of the aims I hope to make a living reality is to fulfil the consortium's flaws. That will show them. Of course, when you do not stand up for anything, you fall for everything else available," he said quietly.

This came as a punch to Xanda, who had been listening intently so far. So, he knew about the ins and outs of the galaxy.

He changed the subject, though.

"But tell me, how did your world end when you guys figured out everything? I bet nothing could destroy your planet. Your civilization is beyond our imagination and something I should like to visit and live in. What happened there?" Xanda asked curiously.

Something was not adding up as far as he was concerned.

Emit smiled at that.

"Well, that is a long story. I will reveal it when the right time comes. I am not sure you are ready for that. However, when such an incident does happen, which it won't, I will be ready for it. The powers that be took us by surprise. We were not ready for it when it happened. The strike was intelligent and clever. Otherwise, we had systems to counter it and could certainly defeat the forces behind it. When that happened, our planet was wiped from existence in a microsecond. Fortunately, I was returning from a mission, which is why I survived. Well, some part of me was gone with the planet. It is a bit complicated how I survived, but I can help you do the same," he explained.

"What do you mean part of you? We have one life. Right?" Xanda asked. By now, he was pretty sure that everything was more twisted on his planet. So, he should keep an open mind instead.

"Not quite. We are evolved beings. Back on my planet, I was tinkering with the body and how it could be separated from the whole. Call it luck or my naughty brain, but I did it. I had discovered a way to recreate life in some event I was destroyed (intentionally or unintentionally). There are more of me hidden in little artefacts across the galaxies in the universe," he said, failing to hide a chuckle.

"And?" Xanda said. He raised his hands in question.

"When I was alive, I was tinkering with human life and what I could do with it. I landed on a novel way of replicating life, which I did and made parts of me. My consciousness is the same, but different parts of me are safely intact across the galaxy, in the far-off recesses of the universe. Only I know where they were and, of course, my father. However, the planet was destroyed and took my father away with it. It was saddening that I had not done it for him and my beloved mother. I can talk to them whenever I want. This part of me you see here is also my work. I would not be standing here without it," he explained.

Xanda took all of this nicely. So, Xanda had several versions of him lying around the universe that he had to access. Maybe that was why he needed his help with everything. He needed his assistance in tying a few things

"Yes. This time you are right. I need some help in lining up some things. Once everything is in place, life will be nothing you have known. Things will be better beyond imagination," he said, gliding to the library.

Xanda saw the life he could have versus the one he was having. It would be a far cry from any of this.

"Okay. I am with you so far. But how did the destruction of your planet come about? Who did it? Have you ever found out? Were the perpetrators punished for their crimes?" he asked innocently.

"Crimes? Punished? Please. It was the Wild Wild West back then. We knew that we were the best. I saw the destruction with my own eyes that fateful day. It happened as I emerged from a wormhole from a mission on another planet. The aim was to gather information on planets we could terraform for others. My father's idea was to provide hospitable conditions to people on different planets. After all, what is the point of living when you cannot do good for others? We saw the disparity across the board and felt guilty. It could not happen like this. Everyone else should have the same rights and lifestyle," he said, looking at Xanda.

He had read Xanda's mind, who had no interest in his altruism. The story was where the fun was for him.

He smiled.

"Right. Sorry. I was staring at a colossal blue star. It was blue in colour. But it was getting bigger. At first, I thought I was imagining things and stood frozen in front of it. Our planet was a mere speck in comparison. But the surprising thing was how did it get there? I knew the stars and solar system trajectory very well. There was nothing scheduled on the calendar as such. And even if that were the case, we would know years ahead. A massive blue star suddenly emerging on our horizon was not something you see every day. I assumed the worst and began realigning my course. Despite being unsure of what I could do, I stayed there. There was no time to alert the space station. Everyone was off duty that day. When I see things in hindsight, it seems someone had eyes on us and attacked us when we least expected it. Someone did not want us," he finished.

This had many questions still.

"Wait. Someone brought a giant star near your planet? How can that happen? Like, how do you bring a giant star?" Xanda asked.

Emit looked at him as if he was joking.

"My dear boy. You live behind the time—too much behind the times. It is very much possible in our realm. I saw the giant star getting larger until it spread over the entire sky. It was heading for critical mass when I realized that it would explode and destroy the entire solar system right that moment. I opened the wormhole slightly—just enough for the spaceship to pass. But leaving like that was not easy. I was leaving everyone behind against my will. Seeing my parents and everything disappear just like that was a sad sight. And then it happened. The blue star exploded into something I cannot describe. It blasted a heap of solar heat and blinding light everywhere—I could see the blast radius to the far recesses of the solar system. There was no time to waste. I hurriedly escaped into the wormhole before the supernova struck a deathly blow. The wormhole closed in the nick of time. As it did, I saw my planet, Centaurus Prime, explode into smithereens. It was a heartbreaking experience and one that I can never forget," he said, reliving the experience.

There was some quiet as the two thoughts about the whole incident.

Xanda was still filling in the blanks here.

"There were no shields on your planet? How is that possible for a civilization like yours?" he asked dismissively.

This angered Emit. However, he composed himself.

"We had shields capable of blocking out a supernova and hypernova. But the problem is that we need someone to man the shields, which were off at the time. I mean, who can predict that someone would land a giant star on the verge of supernova right next to our planet? It does not happen every day," he said, surprised at his assertion.

That much was correct. Someone was truly hellbent on destroying Centaurus Prime; whoever it was certainly had their money's worth considering the spectacle.

He pulled out a book and opened it. The two saw the entire spectacle in front of them. Though for Emit, it was like reliving the past yesterday. He closed his eyes, unable to bear the pain.

It was too much to take.

Xanda put a hand on his shoulder. An icy feeling washed him. He turned away from Xanda and disappeared into the upper shelf of the library.

"I have to get to the bottom of this. That has been my sole mission since the day I reached out to you. I could not access other people for some reason. You somehow connected well to the dreams I was projecting. It was all I could do from here in this chamber. My powers are limited to this chamber. However, with you at the helm, I can now stretch the range of my powers and show what I am capable of. You will forget this consortium forever, as will the other people. I can establish a better society. One that the consortium will be begging to enter," he explained absent-mindedly.

Xanda had one last question here.

"So, what is my role over here?" he asked.

Emit smiled at that. Then he began laughing.

Chapter 6
The Case for God

"What?" he asked.

No response came from him.

"What?" Xanda asked again in annoyance.

Emit was thinking something when he finally spoke.

"I am still working on it. Have not finalized the entire details in this regard. But I will keep you posted when I have it all ready. However, I am still unsure of who did it. There will come a time for revenge; that was for sure. I will not rest until that certain someone is found and dealt with. And that I do very well. I may not need you when the time comes. This is my battle, and I will fight it alone and one-on-one. The powers that will be either destroyed or I will be destroyed in the process. So, I do not wish you to be fodder for my destruction come what may," Emit said, engrossed in his book.

This seemed even odder to Xanda, who wished to see a new day. A new world.

"But you said something about having multiple lives and saving pieces of yourself in the far recesses of the universe? What was that all about then?" he asked.

He certainly wished he had something of the sort as well. Living the life of an immortal as he did was definitely something that could be explored. After all, living as a second-class citizen on a prestigious planet was probably not his cup of tea.

"It should be nobody's cup of tea," Emit said promptly, much to Xanda's annoyance that he had reread his mind.

This time Emit laughed more loudly.

"Trust me, my friend. It is more of a curse than a blessing. I wish our race were not born with this at all. Spending a life like this can be very taxing and traumatizing. You walk around, and everyone's ulterior thoughts are written on their faces. Though it helps figure out people much before you do. I will admit that. But then again, it does not work on alpha races any better, either. Alpha races are superior races in our time. I do not know if they are still here. We had a whole classification system that categorized the races based on their evolutionary trajectory," he said.

Xanda looked a bit blank. What category did he fall in?

Emit tried to hide his laughter.

"Well, we had the Delta category. If I recall correctly, it has been a long time now. This category was the one that could not read minds. The first three categories (alpha, beta, and gamma) could read minds. You can imagine it was a basic quality that the third category of races also possessed," he said dismissively.

This was most interesting. Reading minds was an abysmal quality for the leading races.

However, Xanda had other things on his mind.

"What about the countless lives you have across the universe? Surely, you can use them one after the other. I can join you in this revenge mission," he said helpfully.

Emit had read his mind. Xanda seemed someone hellbent on getting off this ridiculous planet. He seemed to strive for any chance to book the first seat out of here. However, he had no idea about the dangers lurking. He was too naïve for that.

Emit shook his head.

"Nope. Nope. Nope. For now, I do not have the means to recreate you or myself. I found you after much difficulty. This mission becomes near-impossible when you are destroyed with me. Then I have no recourse but to sit out for thousands of years or more before I can find the strength to connect to a living soul. I wish things were not like this. Yet mark my words when we are through this; I will certainly grant you immortality. It is pretty simple. I have been tinkering with our race's DNA for a long time. It is in our genes, but thanks to me, it is transferrable. My world was unfortunately destroyed, and everything else went up in smoke. It will take a while to get everything up and running. Rest assured, with you by my side, I am least worried," he said, closing the book.

Xanda felt his voice softening. Emit maybe not be a bad person, after all. He had been a victim of circumstances. How else would someone react when they have lost everything they loved? He was hanging by a thread here.

His resolve strengthened. "I am up for anything you need. We will do it together and create a world from here onward," Xanda said firmly.

Emit nodded.

He just needed a little coaxing and some deal sweetener to have him on board. Humans were easy. All he had to do was say the right stuff, and they were sold on the very idea. Maybe he could put his plans into motion much earlier than anticipated. However, he had details to work out and draw blueprints in his chamber. But that was a thought for later on.

"Tell me one thing here. How did you find me of all the people in the known universe? And why me? What was so special about me? Is there anything special about me?" he asked.

Emit considered this for a while. Then he looked up.

"My world was way ahead of yours. You very well know that. Similarly, our minds are also evolved beyond your imagination. The planet was entirely blown away. And one part of my consciousness went with it. The more pieces of me, when destroyed, make me weaker. I mean, the extent of my powers becomes weak as more of me is destroyed. I scanned the universe for someone I could reach out to. Do you remember I escaped into the wormhole when the giant star blasted our solar system? This had repercussions that reached far and wide. That hypernova changed the galaxy, blasting half of it away. The radiation then spread into the far recesses of the universe, which created problems for me," he said, bored of the explanation.

Emit thought about bad things coming in threes.

"Problems, how?" Xanda asked.

Emit rolled his eyes.

"Well, the wormhole we can create at will. But there is a limitation to how many times we can do that. And this is random. So, the wormhole threw me into Altius 2.0 galaxy," he explained.

Xanda's blank face told Emit he had no idea about it.

He laughed.

"Your primitive civilization knows the universe till the second layer of the universe. That is only because that is how far your technology allows you to see. We have seen, or should I say, reached the thirtieth layer of the universe. That is the extent of the known universe. You cannot go further than that," he explained.

Xanda was dumbfounded. It seemed that Emit and his peeps had mapped the known universe already.

"Yes, we have. We did that a long time ago. We know every nook and cranny of the universe. For now, the universe is simply expanding into the farther void. Nothing new is happening that we did not know already. Secondly, supernovas and hypernovas provide the change of a new life and also its destruction. In my case, it just blew away half the galaxy and created a vast intergalactic shield. Think of it like a large net. I could access a huge part of the universe because the radiation jammed my signals. The layer still covers a huge section of the universe where communication remains next to impossible. I roamed for a long time, trying to reach out to someone. We had mapped the entire universe, which was very beneficial to me. I had a huge map that was useless for the most part. One half of it was inaccessible, while the other half was pretty much messed up—long story. Your planet was the only one I could reach out to at the time. It was the only one that came on my radar with sentient life," he finished explaining.

Though he had read his mind, Xanda had more questions.

"So, you come into people's dreams? Is that it? I thought you would have a distress signal or something of the sort to reach out to the planet. Maybe even the consortium. They would have helped you easily," Xanda offered.

Emit laughed.

"Can we please change the subject here? I am kind of tired. And no, my spaceship was running on dry fumes. It had exhausted its fuel ages now. I had backup power generation systems that could help me traverse the space. But it cannot power everything. A few compromises must be made," he said, gliding away to the upper shelf.

"Wait a minute. And where did the food come from? I am sure your civilization had food to live and survive. Is that so, or am I in store for more surprises?" he asked.

This was the last question he could think of.

Emit nodded and looked above. Oh, these primitive humans and their questions.

"No. No food for my race. We do not rely on food at all. We have not had food for millions of years. It is not a part of our bodies for millions of years. Our bodies are self-sustainable and thrive on energy created inside our bodies. You may ask how this energy comes to be. This is strange even by my own standards.

Our bodies are composed of this bacteria that thrives on electricity. Electricity is everywhere except your planet. I reckon sometime in the past, these bacteria formed a culture and began active life forms that you see today. That is my reasoning on the matter. But I could be wrong," he explained.

He spoke further.

"I am unsure how or where we came from, evolutionary traits are way above the fold. Over the years, I have noticed that our biological traits are far, far more advanced than beings of our time. However, this day and age are not much different either. We are lucky to be this way," he explained.

Xanda shrugged.

"God knows who or what created you? I mean, what did we do not to deserve all this?" he asked no one in particular.

Emit considered this for a moment.

"My version of God is pretty different from yours. Secondly, you will probably dislike my version of God since yours is too primitive and does not exist. I think yours is a false God. By this logic, I would be a better and more forgiving God in comparison. I read your scripture. I read your mind, so the scripture became pretty obvious to me. I felt sad to see how primitive and ancient people could put someone on a pedestal. It is shocking," he said.

Xanda did not like this, but somewhat he sounded sane.

"And what kind of God do you worship? And may I ask how he is different from my so-called primitive God? Does he have a face? I mean, our God does not believe in presenting him to his people," Xanda said.

Emit beckoned Xanda to follow him.

They rose higher and higher as Emit allowed his hand to dictate the free flow of Xanda in the air. The two went to the topmost shelf, where Emit opened a book, Akhneeda, and beamed.

"I had read your mind long ago, so I knew this question was coming.

"My God remains a mystery to me. It is not a question that your civilization is trying to understand. However, we have been trying to find him in the far recesses of the universe. Sometimes, we feel we come to a roadblock of sorts. This God of mine seems elusive and beyond our comprehension. It remains one of the biggest mysteries of our day. Unlike your God, who has communicated and been there in some shape or form, ours is a mystery. Maybe there is no one there, and that is the beauty of it. I will probably get to this when we are done with this mission," Emit explained.

"So, basically, your God does not exist?" Xanda asked stupidly.

Emit shook his head.

"No. You are not getting it. It is not a he/she or something of that sort. It is something indescribable and complex. We have received signs at different points. Those signs I still remember. But I know that it is not a person," he concluded.

Xanda nodded and thought it pointless to argue further.

Chapter 7
Back to the Civilization

Then Xanda realized he was late for a thing he had to do. He tapped his wrist for a response.

Nothing happened.

He slapped it a few times, but nothing happened.

"Come on. Come on. Why is it not working?" he asked in mild agony.

Emit stood there laughing.

"You are in the disappearing library, Xanda. What did you expect?" he said matter-of-factly.

"What do you mean by that? The disappearing library is on my planet. Of course, everything should work as it does. Am I right?" he felt a bit unsure now.

Emit shook his head.

"Nope. Not exactly. And who told you that the disappearing library is on your planet? May I ask?" he asked a little condescendingly.

Xanda just shrugged. It was maybe time for another explanation from this guy.

He shook his head.

"My dear boy! The disappearing library does not exist on your planet. It does not exist on any other planet. No one is that for it. It is something that is beyond the space-time continuum. So, it exists outside our realm. You can call the disappearing library just about anywhere, and it will be there. I have sought its honoured existence in the far recesses of the universe when I have been trapped. One time, a dragon's giant jaws were nearly on my head. I summoned the disappearing library, and I was in there in a moment. I could not breathe for a bit when I returned to the library. It was just a spur-of-the-moment thing. It was then I realized it appeared anywhere and at any time. Times have been dangerous and life-threatening, but the disappearing library has always been there to save my neck. It is your God, but better," he said, chuckling a bit.

He stood a little silently. Xanda spoke up.

"Anyhow, I will see you later. Have to get some things straightened out here," he said, staring at something in the distance.

As Xanda blinked once, Emit was there. He had disappeared by the next blink. How did he do that?

Xanda shrugged. He remembered an errand he had to run back to his planet. Okay. It was time to get out.

He closed his eyes, hoping he would open his eyes to his planet. He had not asked how to leave the disappearing library. Entering had been a fluke as well.

I want to be on my planet, he thought.

He opened his eyes with relief. The fresh morning wind kissed him, bringing a smile to his face. Ahhhhh. The sound of the home is always welcome and refreshing.

Bam!

He was thrown away, much to his surprise.

"Cripes. What the hell is wrong with you?" he shouted to no one in particular. Someone sped away, disappearing as quickly as he had appeared.

As he opened his eyes, he was left dumbstruck.

"What is this place? Dear Lord. I have no idea where I am," he said in shock.

This place was something else. The planet had considerably changed while he was gone. Everything seemed new and unfamiliar to him.

In anger, he slapped his wrist for his computer to buzz in. However, it was as dead as a fish. What the hell is wrong with this thing? Why is it not working?

His wrist beeped ever so slightly.

"Frequency changed to 90 T-GHz," the sound said as it clicked off.

His eyes opened in surprise. What the heck is a T-GHz frequency? As he remembered, his planet worked on a frequency of 100 MHz for communication and transportation devices. His planet had conformed with the system established by the consortium (Galaxy Confederation of Races) that aimed to have a unified system for all the other planets. It was a standard system to bring the worlds inside the consortium up to speed with systems for a good life. Furthermore, the 100 MHz frequency band allowed immediate connectivity with the database systems, electronica, and teleportation of spaceships from deep space.

So, as things stood, Xanda was left stranded in the middle of nowhere and had nowhere to go. His planet seemed foreign to him. The people could be seen hovering high above him. So, they had transitioned upward.

"God! What will I ever do here? He kept slapping his wrist in anger for it to work. But all it got was the same response again and again.

"System error. Frequency mismatched! Frequency mismatch," the sound came.

He looked around for some clue. Things had changed drastically from when he had left the planet for a few moments. He felt a bit angered. Emit should have told him about the dynamics of the disappearing library and its effect on the space-time continuum. This seemed the future. Which year, he was unsure. That remained to be determined. Though the fact that Emit was solely concerned with his goals, for the most part, did not help matters much. It somewhat angered him. The moment he had entered his life, things had felt different. He barely commented on things other than his mission.

He supposedly stood on his planet, which had drastically changed from when he left.

"What is this place?" he shouted.

No one answered because he was all alone here on the ground.

Yet to his surprise, a spotlight fell on him. He looked around, but nothing was visible at this height. As he looked above him, he realized what had happened.

His planet, as he remembered, had a very much different landscape. It was now based high in the sky above. He strained to see a bit more. His eyes could see the light whizzing past in quick succession. As he took stock of the situation, sprawling structures could be seen high above him. He saw them moving around mid-air and thought about him miserably down below.

This was very weird.

At that moment, he disappeared from where he stood.

The next moment he was standing inside what looked like a prison. The two clues he got that he was now a prisoner were:

➤ Inmate # 000.000.312

➤ He was wearing a black jumpsuit

He felt disgusted by being treated as a criminal on his own planet. Like what, a few centuries had passed, and he would be treated that way? That was so not on. At least, the authorities could have rechecked his status when he had arrived or something of the sort.

"State your name for the record, alien," a law enforcement official said in a severe tone.

It took him by surprise.

"I am not an alien. Wait. I am not a criminal. Just check my records first. I cannot believe I am standing here in prison. This is insane," he stammered.

The law enforcement official did not seem to hear a thing.

"And name your planet and reason for arrival here. Remember! Anything you say off-handed can be used against you in a court of law with video evidence. So, I suppose you should be honest and think before you speak. We have to process political refugees, bounty hunters, aliens, and people seeking asylum," he said in a monotone.

Xanda was stumped. What was he even on about? Though the reality of things was beginning to set.

"Wait, what? Do your records say something? I will come on them. Type my name. Xanda. The interplanetary ID is 7220. Please do that before you return. I have to be somewhere today and resolve some pressing matters. It is of paramount importance," Xanda finished.

The law enforcement official looked at him like he was stupid or something.

"No, no, no. Son, you are staying here forever in this cell. You have nothing to get you out. Nothing until we know something about you or your motive on this planet. Remember, if nothing comes on you, we will deport you to the interplanetary prison where all those enrolled have no record. I have a feeling you might go there. Nothing is showing on my records. See you later," he finished leaving the door.

Xanda stood there, thinking of his options. Could Emit bail him out somehow? He was unsure of that. Could he escape from here somehow? Though this jail cell was not the one that looked similar to one in another life when he last visited.

The jail cell was an odd one. He took four steps, trying to walk out of prison. Though he knew it would not be possible. An invisible force blocked him. A weird sound greeted him as soon as he exceeded his confines.

"That is odd. They have some shield to prevent prisoners from escaping," he muttered.

As he looked around, he saw that the prison complex was overly massive. It went as high as he could see. Some prisoners were idling around while others were looking at the latest inmate in prison. The cellblock had rows and rows of prisoners wearing the same black jumpsuit.

This was getting frustrating, he thought.

He banged the invisible shield. Maybe something would happen, he thought. Upon the third strike, he was thrown backwards with immense force. He fell face first. This reminded him of when he fell on his face on the stairs as a child. His legs felt like spaghetti as he struggled to stand up. He saw some of the inmates laughing there hysterically.

"Shut up! I said, shut up," he shouted.

I have an idea.

A fellow inmate beside him in the other cell was watching him with disinterest. A look of humour crossed the face.

Then he realized. This was astonishing! He was near a living and breathing dragon. However, this dragon was much smaller in size. His scaly skin was all black, while its white eyes looked dreadful. As he breathed in and out, some greyish smoke emerged. Maybe his stomach was storing fire inside.

"Can we talk for a while? What is this place? How long are you booked here for?" he asked him.

The dragon moved his small hands to indicate that he could not hear him. Then he also indicated that the prison complex does not allow talk with the prisoners. Every prisoner was allowed his company to enjoy. However, exceptions could be made when someone was a model prisoner.

Nice dragon, he thought.

He sat down thinking about that. God! How he would ever complete Emit's mission was beyond him. On second thought, he also thought about his future.

At this moment, the law enforcement guy returned.

"Well, we do not have anything about you on the records. No criminal or civil records. No matching identity. No nothing. It is almost as if you entered here. Although how did you arrive here still beats me. We are deporting you to the interplanetary prison. It is for those who have no record or identity of any sort. The system will take you there in a few moments.

Poof!

He was standing in a very dilapidated prison on someone's face.

"Get off me," the man shouted.

Xanda stepped away, feeling sheepish.

This was getting worse at the moment.

At that moment, Emit appeared.

Emit stood there, trying not to laugh.

"Can you get me the hell out of here? I am serious. Please let me out," Xanda screamed.

This made him laugh more.

"You clearly do not remember a thing I told you. Maybe you are hopeless. I should find someone else to take on this mission. I need a person who can think on his feet. You are not that person," Emit said coldly.

Xanda turned around—this was it. He was done with Emit. God knows how long he sat there when Emit spoke.

"I am kidding. You are something. I made the right decision to select you for the mission. Now turn around and talk to me," he said warmly.

Xanda almost turned but then decided against it.

"Oh. Come on. Please do not give me that. I was messing around. You could have broken out of the previous jail cell as well. As I said, you did not think hard enough. If you had, you would have escaped long ago and returned to your own planet," he finished, checking something on his wrist.

"And what is that I should not have thought about?" Xanda said, still turning to the other side.

"The disappearing library," he announced silently.

Xanda turned around then. It was the first time there was a surprise on his face.

Surely, I could have thought of that.

It was all coming back to him. The disappearing library helped Emit once escape the jaws of death. I could have easily escaped from the jail cell when I wished for the disappearing library.

"Yes. You could have escaped right then," Emit said, reading his mind.

"Stop reading my mind," Xanda protested.

Emit did not answer this. The guy seemed edgy already.

"So, are you ready to leave?" he asked glumly.

Xanda nodded—he was tired of this place already. It felt like someone had taken a dump here. People were shouting at law enforcement officials. It was like living in a primitive society.

Emit had disappeared before he could say yes.

"Yeah. Yeah. Pull the disappearing act on me," he complained.

He closed his eyes for a while, hoping it would happen again. It was a fluke. If he did it this time, it would be on his own.

He opened his eyes. Voila!

He was standing in the disappearing library once again.

"You did it," came a familiar voice from behind.

Chapter8
Sins of the Father

"Welcome back, dear Xanda," Emit said, raising his arms in an embrace. It seemed as if he was happy to see him, meeting him after a long time.

He hated the mere sight of Emit at this moment. Who does that to a friend?

"Yeah. Yeah. Just keep it quiet for a while. I want to process my thoughts about stuff," he said, looking at the sprawling library.

Emit looked at him.

"And do not read my mind. Just let it be for a while," he said, fuming. This was an afterthought because Emit had read his mind quite earlier.

"Yes. I see that you do not like me. Maybe it was because of the incidents in prisons back-to-back. That is somewhat your fault. I was back here waiting for you to think of the disappearing library and prompt arrival here. However, when that did not happen, I stepped in to help you. Albeit it was fun to see you as you were. You see how your kind treats you," he said, lighting up.

Xanda raised an eyebrow here.

"Wait. Were you enjoying my misery back there? Is that it? I am going back. From the moment we began this journey, you have been nothing but selfish and, like a moron, went on and on about your planet. I have had enough. I thought you were my friend. But clearly, you see enjoyment and fulfilment in other people's misery. Goodbye, Emit or whatever your name is. I hope you find what you are looking for, but this should be a two-way street," he said, closing his eyes.

Opening his eyes, he would be back on his planet. He missed the smell of his planet's air. But this time, he had an idea. He would request the disappearing library to send him back to his timeline, where he knew his people. He knew life was great on his planet, albeit it was not perfect. It had its flaws. But it was better than what Emit was offering. He felt that leaving him was a bad thing. After all, he would be stranded in this library until he could carry out his plan. Maybe Emit should have been more careful then. He deserved more than cheap thrills at his expense.

Emit was laughing for a while. Xanda stole a glance noticing that he was not worried about his untimely departure from the disappearing library. His departure did not seem to worry him.

Xanda opened his eyes, yet he was still in the disappearing library.

"Welcome back. You cannot leave the library until I feel you can. It is a bit early for that," Emit said.

Xanda opened his eyes. He was livid. Was he a prisoner over here, trapped for eternity until Emit had his minion doing the work? Was he really that crass?

"No, no, no. You are not here for an eternity. That is not my purpose for doing that. As soon as you are done with the mission here, I will give you a choice to live with me on my planet or return to your timeline. The choice will always be yours. Although once you live on my planet, there is no going back. Life on my planet is so good. I can give a tour when the time comes," he said as if reading Xanda's mind.

The deal was not that bad.

"So, I am a prisoner here, I take it?" he asked, skipping his monologue.

"Yes and no. It depends on how you look at it. I see you as a friend and someone here helping me when I was unable to," he said.

Xanda saw some humour here.

"A prisoner friend, if you may then," Xanda said.

"And no, I cannot feel happiness, misery, or those tumultuous feelings you felt. As I have said, we are an evolved race that grew out of these emotions during the ancient time of our race. We have acquired the ability to see the past, present, and future, so things are different from how I see them," he finished.

He had Xanda's attention now.

"Wait. You can see the future and the past. Like how is that even possible? Who the hell can do that? We were working on a time machine that could access the future. Although the idea of accessing the past sounds appealing to me more," he recalled some work he had come across on his planet.

Emit laughed a bit more at that.

"Yes. I am aware of that. It was a pity to see your people still at sixes and sevens at working that thing out. However, we do not need machines/devices to go there. We access the past and future all the time without any device/machine. This is why I came across you. I see a future where I will live in the disappearing library for eternity. That is not something I want. Do I? You are here to shape my future. With your assistance, I can revive my planet. Reviving is not the exact plan. But something I will do to restart life on my planet. The disappearing library is my refuge for now, as it is yours. I have some parts of my existence scattered across the universe. So, I will access them as well, and then I am all set," he explained.

This was amazing. He could see the past.

"And what do you see in my past?" Xanda asked before he stopped himself.

Emit was staring at some bookshelf.

"What is there to know? You were thrown on this planet by some bounty hunters when your planet needed a labour force to man the engines. After that, you have lived here mostly treading the waters. Your parents are unknown to you because they never saw you. It would be painful to know that your parents sold you on this black market. And although selling children was illegal on their home planet. However, your parents went ahead and did it. How do I know? I know because I read your mind. You may not recall it because you were a newborn then. Oh, and those bounty hunters arrived on this planet and made a marginal profit on your sale. They were doing that during the initial phase of the planet's habitation. Sickening as it is, it is what happened. Am I correct?" he asked Xanda.

A tear rolled, though he tried to hide it. And nodded.

Emit smiled at that.

"As I said, our race was well ahead of time. How did it happen? I do not know, but I can find out. Your race only sees in the present, which was common in primitive races of my day. We can see in the past just as well as in the future. Of course, changing them is impossible unless we have the tools for it. My future mostly involves me living here and exploring the contents of the disappearing library. I have explored other places. As you very well know that the disappearing library can take you anywhere. I was here for a long time, and during this time, I explored the far recesses of the space. Galaxies upon galaxies and different star systems, hoping that someday some planet could be something similar I want. Unfortunately, that search is still on," he finished, sounding slightly sad.

Xanda stood there, wondering who would have created this race of superhumans. Their abilities were beyond those of the ordinary people in his star system. Their creator would be something beyond imagination.

"He is something beyond my imagination as well. Imagine how his abilities would be when we have abilities that exceed your imagination, no matter how you stretch them. This gives me an idea. Did you know my dad disappeared, searching for the creator who created our race? Let us proceed to the topmost shelf of the disappearing library. My dad, on this journey, wrote a book. The good thing is that it ends where he last disappears, so we know where he left. And it is not just a book about his time in space. It packs quite a lot because space missions are dull and dreary," he said as the two glided towards the topmost shelf.

Xanda was surprised that he was floating in the air at a moderate speed. He looked at Emit, who just looked and smiled at that.

"Of course, one of the many abilities I have. Ordinarily, I https://projectcamp.io/task-detail?id=KnlPqheqsjwould have been a God on your planet had I revealed myself. But I am not as selfish as you think. I could do that anytime I want for infinite star systems. But I feel that is wrong. I could not live with myself if I had done that. My race had telekinesis powers, meaning we could move ourselves and objects regardless of size. It was the perks of our God that were kind to us and shaped us in his image," he beamed.

The two came to the topmost shelf. As Xanda stared at the ground level, his vision blurred slightly. It was as if the ground floor did not even exist.

"Why can I not see anything?" he asked, pretty sure that he had just left the ground.

"You cannot see anything from here because your eye is too primitive to see such interstellar distances. Its range is too limited," he explained.

Xanda looked at him with the same stupid face Emit found humorous.

"Yes. Interstellar distances. You see, the topmost shelf is far away from the ground level. Your planet does not have the technology to reach above here, even if they reach here somehow. I can do that, or my race if it were here. How else do you know I visited different planets, galaxies, and star systems to see if something was worth my while?" he asked him.

Xanda shrugged.

"By wishing for a planet like yours?" he offered.

Emit did not take that well.

"And you think I had not tried that all the time I have lived here?" he said, roaring throughout the library.

Xanda shrugged again. It was better to stay quiet.

As he opened the book, his father stood there beaming in his spacesuit. His attire was shaded differently.

"Hello there, son. How has it been? Sad that my mission ended here. I was only inches away from finding Maximus," he said to Emit.

Emit did a weird ceremonial bow in front of him and circled for what Xanda did not know why nor care.

His father turned to Xanda, who waved a hand. Emit quickly stood in front of him.

"He is just a friend I picked along the way. Hopefully, I will recreate life on our planet with his help. I am not sure of a few things. But it is a start," he said firmly.

His dad nodded and seemed silent for a moment. Xanda was clueless about the ensuing silence.

"Dad, I want to go through your failed mission. Although it was a success, your disappearance has people still baffled. Feel free to clue us in about it," he said nonchalantly.

He nodded.

"What part do you wish to know? I have it all right here," he said.

"I want to know about the God we follow," he said.

His dad did not seem much impressed by that choice. He thought for a while.

Tense moments passed. Emit smiled at Xanda.

"Well, then, as you wish. As part of a book, I am also bound by some rules. Our God's name is Maximums Glorious. However, significantly less is known about him. However, I will expand because I had some interaction with him during the missions. You would be surprised to know that he was once a mortal man. As primitive as the guy standing behind you. He breathed and died like everyone else. However, a dying God clung to him and changed the man. This dying God (Titania) was on her last leg when Maximus was leaving the planet. Cosmic being as she was, she was turning to dust. Trust me; it is nearly impossible to get rid of her. She possesses your body and takes over your mind and body. The dying God, as we would come to know, had a massive appetite. Her planet was empty of sentient life for a reason. I reckon someone had left her there for eternity. Upon possessing his body, she began devouring yet again. Moons became planets and then whole stars. The witch was unknown to people, maybe forgotten in the annals of history. Maximus had little control of his mind and body when she took over. He realized nothing was enough for her. She consumed star systems like an appetizer. His entry would spell disaster for new planets and galaxies. You see, winters would prevail wherever she would go. Life became inhabitable as a slow death came upon them. It was her way of finishing everything on her path. Planets, star systems, and galaxies became ice when she passed. This would go on as Maximus remained a prisoner in his own body. Titania ate the far recesses of the universe. This was fine for some because the space outskirts had little life. The fringe aliens and bounty hunters infested these areas," he explained.

This was interesting. As far as Xanda knew, his God had told less about him. He preferred to remain anonymous. The less his people knew, the better.

"Is there a way to stop him then?" Xanda asked.

Emit's dad nodded.

"So, in a way, he can die if he ceases to consume planets like he did all the time back then. That was his only source of energy. Consuming a star once in a while was enough for a long time. When that happened, he would disappear for long periods. Although he was the last descendant of his race, he never revived them or brought them back. However, he had a change of heart later on when he lost vast cosmic amounts of energy in a freak accident. That slowed him down for a while," his dad explained.

"Why?" Emit and Xanda both asked.

"He managed to kill Titania. This was a strange development in his life. It is something he cannot explain either. However, it happened. But things were not as simple as that. She had died but left her devouring power inside him. So, he could do anything of his accord except for the devouring part. He struggled with that. He created his own star system, where he lived for the rest of his days. The star system was a feared one. No one came closer to or even thought of passing it during some errands or space mission. It would devour anything in its path. There was a reason its environs were empty and devoid of anything. It had consumed everything in its path, maintaining a force field near-impossible to break through," his dad continued.

There was muted silence between the three. Emit, and Xanda thought of these incidents to themselves before dad broke the silence.

"To this day, we do not know where Maximus Glorious is because he felt the power he had was too all-consuming. In the wrong hands, it would wipe out the entire universe. His whereabouts are largely unknown. This is my reasoning about him because he disappeared without a trace. And get this, we know the deep and far voids of the universe. If he vanished, he did a good job of it," he concluded, beaming at the end.

Xanda was listening intently so far. One question still remained. How did Emit's race come into existence?

"Good question, primitive alien. Maximus had laid waste to countless star systems and galaxies when he was possessed. He created a race that was something else. And we were born in his image. He gave us the abilities that we had, and so generously used them. Some of these are much-needed, and I wonder if we can live without them. Teleportation and levitation are some useful powers. It took a small ounce of his infinite energy to create us because, as we all know, his power accumulated is beyond our comprehension. Creating planets, resurrection, travelling at light speed, and of course, telepathy. We are almost Gods on your primitive planet. I can sense your disbelief," his dad shrugging.

Xanda thought this was odd of a God to be so generous and kind.

"He was generous and kind. After all, he was a mortal man and wished the best. His aim was to devour more planets so he could raise his previous race. For that, he would have to repeat the course of the one he had killed, which conflicted with his humanness. He then disappeared abruptly. No one knows where. Our race frequently talked to him as he visited the planet from time to time and offered suggestions. Remember: He had not bestowed us with all the powers, fearing the same end he saw firsthand. His generosity was astronomical. He made it a point to cease devouring worlds while raising many from the dead. This was an energy-exhaustive process, due to which we saw less and less of him. Eventually, he disappeared one fine day when we woke up. He was nowhere to be found. His last message was to be good to primitive races because we had an obvious advantage over others. However, he seems less worried because, of course, he can see the future. With that message, he was gone from our lives forever," his dad said.

Xanda was hooked. It had been an interesting turn of events thus far.

"And did you disappear then?" Xanda asked, realizing it was a tricky question.

His dad laughed at that.

"I was chasing a trail left by Maximus. He was secretive about it, but I was the only one chasing that. Chasing him brought me quite outside our normal space-time continuum. My system went blank for the most part. This is the last thing I can recall. And that is where Emit comes in!" his dad replied.

Chapter 9
The Big Freeze

Emit and Xanda stood staring at him. Indeed, there was more to it than that. They could not be grasping at straws here.

Emit's dad realized that.

"Oh. And I have the flight plan right here, so you can replicate my course right until my disappearance. That will be easy to do. The spaceship is pretty self-reliant. You just have to sit inside. It will chart the course itself and gauge the usual path before setting off. You do not need to lift a finger unless necessary," he reasoned.

Again, there was more silence as Xanda and Emit looked at him for further instructions.

"And no, I do not know if you will find me somewhere along the way—that information I do not have. Anyhow, we have reached the end of this book. So, there you go. Make me proud, son. It would certainly be great to see Maximus in all his glory. We came from him, and there is so less that we know of him. The more I know, the more I am fascinated by him. So far, the stuff I know about him is just the tip of the iceberg. There was more to the character than meets the eye. I often wonder if he knew I was hot on his tail when he disappeared. Of course, he would know that. He was a God, but I am unsure. He was full of surprises, to the point of surprising himself sometimes. There could be something deep-seated for his disappearance. I can never rest until

I see him or, at the very least, have a word with him," he murmured.

Emit had an idea.

"You can join us on the journey, you know," Emit said, stifling a chuckle.

His dad thought for a moment and then beamed.

"I never thought of that. So, when are we leaving?" he prompted the question.

Emit looked at Xanda, who nodded.

"We are ready whenever you are. Of course, Xanda will be surprised to see your holographic version travelling with us into deep space. It is not possible in this day and age. But then again, so much more is not possible. His civilization has limitations," he explained to his dad.

Xanda raised an eyebrow. Surely, he could appreciate his being here, of all things.

"I do appreciate you being here," said Emit, much to Xanda's annoyance.

"Yes. I can see that. He comes from a very, very primitive civilization. I wonder if we could ever live the way he does and do as much as we can with so many obvious shortcomings," his dad said somewhat condescendingly.

"Okay. Okay. Enough of the mudslinging at my civilization. I am the only reason you can revive your planet or whatever. And I am the only reason your dad will accompany you on this journey. Otherwise, good luck staying trapped in this book of yours. It must be fun, right? Xanda said, visibly annoyed.

He heard his dad laughing. However, Emit found no humour in it. He knew Xanda was right.

"Yes. You heard it. Either you can stay in the library or learn to appreciate my worth here. Your son here found me to help him with the mission. So, maybe get off your high horses for once. And truth be told, your civilization is thankless and full of yourself. Maybe Maximus left for more humble and thankful people because you feel self-centred," Xanda roared.

This left Emit and his dad silent. Xanda thought this should be given a reality check. For someone far advanced in everything, they did lack etiquette.

"That is not true," dad replied. It surprised Xanda.

"Let me explain. Our people are different from your kind of people. These variables I read in your mind were non-existent in our day and age. I want to learn when all this is over. Maybe that is why I reckon you dislike us," his dad explained.

Xanda was looking elsewhere. He just did not need any explanation from these two. Maybe some people were better off dead. His dad or whatever his name was no better than Emit.

"Callahan. The name is Callahan," Emit's dad replied quietly.

He continued.

"If it is any consolation and the mission is successful, I suppose you can live with us on the planet. It is something you have never experienced before. I mean, the possibilities we can open for you are limitless. You have an idea about Emit's capabilities. Imagine having that for yourself. Maybe you can return to your planet and implement your learning there. We happened to be destroyed in the process, unbeknownst to us. By whom I do not know," his dad said.

Xanda nodded. As if this was not clear enough to him already. It was all about them and them alone when Xanda entered their lives. His discomfort with their selfishness prompted them to offer some consolatory prize. Ugh.

Surprisingly, no answer came from the two. Xanda was well aware that they could read his mind. It was a gift they had, thanks to their God.

Emit had already left. He was preparing for the mission his father had bestowed upon him. As he saw, he had disappeared into the other side of the library, his face deep into another book. Callahan stood there watching though Xanda thought he knew what his son was doing.

After a few moments, Emit returned with a beaming smile while presenting the title *Infinite Corridors: A Brief History of the Unknown.*

"I have got this. We will use the Infinite Corridors. It will be quicker and faster, and I feel we will land on the cusp of our civilization. Have you heard of this, my father?" he asked Callahan.

He shook his head.

"Nope. I had never heard of it. I think you have done well here. I should get out more and explore this library. So, what is the portal about?" he asked Emit.

Emit nodded.

"I am glad you asked," he said.

"The *Infinite Corridor* is an alternate realm that gives momentary access to many different worlds independent of space and time. This means it is not governed by space or time. It is independent of it. Think of it as a bridge linking different worlds and dimensions along a straight path. Some call it an endless tunnel. No one has fully reached the end of the tunnel if it has an end. The knowledge of the tunnel was only known to a select few dark theurgists until it was buried with them. It is arcane knowledge first recorded after the arrival of a band of theurgists and sorcerers that briefly wreaked havoc, entering and leaving planets and plundering places. They entered these same corridors and left, mostly sending wild warmongers like humongous Androids, mighty energy hydras, and enormous monoliths animated via quantum micro-machines to lay waste after their departure. These things were nearly impossible to kill. Bows, arrows, and primitive weapons did not work on them. They were dark creatures, so only magic could defeat these ungodly beings. Where the theurgists went or what became of them is subject to speculation. No one saw or heard from them again. Fortunately, the dark creatures also faded into dust because magic is not eternal. It has a life and needs revival. The planets are in a system we know as S1-Prime. A slew of planets within the immediate and nearby solar systems remains dry and barren to this day. Efforts to inhabit them have been difficult due to the presence of dark magic. Space missions lost contact with their home planets post-entering their atmosphere until missions were abandoned. So the place where these planets are located is known as the *Destruction Belt*. It is off limits as per the space travel protocols," Emit read.

Xanda was fascinated by this story. He was missing out so much had he been on his planet.

Emit smiled, looking at Xanda.

"Anyhow, back to the *Infinite Corridor*. Many believe that the *Infinite Corridor* is nothing more than a fairytale. They open with some weird dark incantations in a language spoken by those arcane theurgists. The words for the incantation are these," Emit spoke them in a high pitch.

Suddenly, a purple void began opening, showcasing a longish bridge that seemed to go forever. Xanda looked at Emit, who shook his head. They were not entering right now.

The void began closing as soon it began to open, becoming smaller and smaller until it disappeared.

"The doors to the often called 'fabled corridor' are sparse and habitually flicker in and out of plain sight. Opening the portal is excruciatingly taxing, requiring herculean mental effort. It says over here that the arcane theurgists crucified the commoner until the door opened for a very short window. It is alleged that the large warmongers left behind could be a ploy to open the door because it requires sentient sacrifice. Some alchemy is also required in the right balance, although not always necessary. One eyewitness account alleges he saw the spirits of dead bodies disappearing into some fiery creature, leaving just the skeletons of the bodies behind. He adds that this fiery creature was high in the sky and vanished into thin air after the deed was done. It was scary to be the only person left behind. However, it was tough to fend off the dark creatures. They roamed the planet all day long. They did not sleep or eat anything. The only purpose they seemingly have is destruction. He may die soon because there is nothing left to hide behind," Emit said.

He stared at Callahan and Xanda. The two had their mouths open.

"We are not done here. There is more to this. Trust me. It gets weirder and weirder," he noted.

"However, it remains to be seen whether the *Infinite Corridor* exists or was destroyed in some event. It has been aeons since the fabled portal was reopened. The recent history does not report any sightings of this sort, nor have any theurgists emerged thus far. This further makes the whole story a mystery itself. The disappearance of the arcane theurgists remains a mystery to this day. Maybe someone someday will find them inside the corridor or some distant world. The cursed theurgists were the only ones in recorded history to open such a fabled portal, tearing the fabric of reality, as they say. Others allege the story as a complete fabrication, pointing out that the so-called *Destruction Belt* or anything close to it has not been found inside the solar system. They are quick to note that explorers have tried to locate the *Destruction Belt,* much to their annoyance. A string of destroyed planets inside the said solar systems remains as much a mystery as the theurgists and the corridor itself," he said. He paused for a while.

"The portal is much like another fabled Disappearing Library that can appear anywhere and at any time. Also alleged as a fabrication, the library's origin is a mystery that remains unanswered even today," he said, digressing.

Xanda's eyes widened. Maybe this library was not a mystery as much.

Emit continued.

"When you are inside the mythical corridor, different worlds open and close. The timeframe is little, so better to jump in before the window to the world closes. There is no telling when your world will reappear and after how long. The corridor works at random, making it undesirable for some. There is no telling about how many worlds and dimensions are inside and if the tunnel itself ends somewhere," he noted.

"Opening the portal requires immense energy dissipation. Those wielding incredible dark power or dark resources will rev the engines of the fabled corridor, firing it up again. It requires herculean focus to control the engines of this corridor accurately. According to one theurgist, it took him a few years to regain his dark ability after returning from the corridor. His dark skills declined monumentally after repeated visits. He says it was like living like a shadow of his former self. The origin of the mythical corridor remains a mystery to this day. No account or information about how it came to exist. As odd as it sounds, the fabled corridor and arcane theurgists appear and disappear together. The corridor is blood-coloured on the inside, spinning continuously like some engine is working it. The longish tunnel goes on endlessly while different worlds open and close on either side. There is no order to these worlds, as each springs up for no rhyme or reason.

On the other hand, someone trying to find his desired world would be hard-pressed to locate one. After all, they appear randomly inside the tunnel. So, there is no telling when your world will appear or ever return. That remains to be seen," Emit said, closing the book.

He seemed exhausted from reading this story.

"This was one hell of a story," Xanda said, sounding intrigued.

Callahan nodded.

"I remember we never needed something mythical like corridors to reach corners of the space," his dad opined.

This made Xanda laugh for the first time.

Callahan shrugged.

"And we would have done so without bloodshed or leaving behind a trail of death and destruction. This just seems too barbaric and inhumane for my taste. It was better that these theurgists were wiped off eventually. Otherwise, everyone would be dead or something," he said in dismay.

Emit nodded.

"There is no time to waste. Let me repeat the incantations, and the corridor will open. When that happens, I want everyone to jump inside. However, I am not sure if we will find our own planet once inside and how long that takes is also unclear. We will eventually find our planet by hit and trial. And yes, you can return to your planet if you like. That is your choice. I trapped you for the duration of the portal, or I could find it. However, now that the task is complete, we can do without you," he said casually.

Xanda nodded.

"I am coming with you. There is no point in returning to the planet and living my life," he said, shrugging.

Emit and Callahan nodded.

As he spoke the incantations, the portal began opening again. This time, it was wider and showed different worlds everywhere.

"Come on. Jump now," Emit said.

The two jumped first, followed by Emit the last. The portal closed, and now they were inside the *Infinite Corridor*.

"My God! This is wonderful. And how do we leave this place?" Xanda asked.

Emit smiled at that. "Nothing. Just repeat these incantations, and we will be back inside the library," he said.

Callahan had an idea.

"Let us do one thing. We will stand here and wait for our world to appear. When that happens, we will jump immediately. And if Emit is asleep, I will levitate him to the planet," he said.

They waited for how long they lost count.

When Xanda woke up, he was left astounded. A colossal object the size of the sun was drawing closer. This was different.

The sun seemed to have frozen while unbelievably closer to Emit's planet. It seemed odd. He looked around.

The vast space around him was turned bluish everywhere.

"What is that?" he asked Emit, dumbfounded.

"It is what you call ice. The solar system has turned into ice, but how, I have no idea," he said, plain as white.

This changes my plan a bit, he thought.

Chapter 10
On a Collision Course

"Will you please tell me what the hell is happening here?" Xanda asked in irritation. Maybe he could die at this moment while these two were mum.

Callahan stared blankly at the massive star, clearly lost for an explanation. They were like a speck in the sky near it. The size of the star was so enormous that it covered the entire view in front of them. It seemed to be drawing closer and closer. Or maybe they were drawn towards it by its gravity.

"There is no time to explain here. I am trying to figure it out. Just shut the hell up for a while. You do realize that the sun will blow us away in a few moments, and you want an explanation here?" he roared at Xanda.

Maybe it could wait! After all, he would die first instead of these two.

He pushed him out of the control room and moved his head slightly. This locked the door, shutting Callahan and Xanda out.

Callahan spoke first.

"I think I may have an idea what happened here. Just a piece of the puzzle, not the whole puzzle," Callahan said, hovering over to the nearest window where the colossal star seemed deathly. Massive explosions on the star's surface were visible from this distance. Xanda noticed the star was greenish in colour and, indeed, many times more massive than the star housed in their solar system. This was something else entirely.

Callahan was standing near the window, completely impassive, staring at the sun.

"This could be dangerous. The explosions from the sun could alone destroy us, let alone the star nearing the end of its natural life cycle. You see, these explosions keep the star up and running. It is like an engine that needs fuel. This fuel comes from the typical cosmic elements of Helium and Hydrogen. I am afraid if we near the star a bit more, some of the explosions will blow the spaceship away. I am unsure if we have the capability of surviving an explosion the size of this star in front of me. My son tells me that this was what drove us to extinction. That is alarming to me, given that I thought we were immortal, made in the image of Maximus. Clearly, that is not the case here. I certainly cannot die here because I am a holographic image, but my son is very much alive," he said, talking to himself more than Xanda.

Xanda had other things on his mind, in any case.

"And why is the solar system frozen in bluish ice? What happened here, and who did it? How can someone pull this off?" he asked, staring at the rear window where a frozen landscape greeted his eyes.

The blue ice stretched as far as his eyes could see. This was new for him, seeing far-off planets and distant galaxies turned into ice and flying meteorites and asteroids turned blue, emitting cold fumes. Just the thought made Emit shiver.

Callahan began to explain.

"Well, it is simple. One of the leading theories of the universe's death is the Big Freeze, also called the Big Chill. You see, the universe we made was not perfect in design. It was haphazardly made without much forethought or future planning. Be that as it may, the universe will never cease to expand. It will continue going through a cycle of deaths and rebirths, which is a part of its design. Initially, if we were to remain alive, we would have experienced these rebirths and deaths live. However, that did not happen, so here we are. As per this theory, the end of the universe is a long and cold affair. There will come a time when the universe will cease expanding as it does naturally. Its system will begin working against itself. We have known this for some time and had systems in place to counteract it. The Big Freeze is simply happening. The core reason is due to a lack of energy to work with and heat in the system overall. When stars collapse under their own gravity, they blow up and blast their solar systems out of existence. Over time, this will increase as the stars reach the end of their life cycles. However, with the distances ever increasing due to this inefficient system, the energy will dissipate and fail to form new stars and solar systems in the previous one's stead. Call this slow poison or the snake eating its own eggs. The system begins to freeze due to the absence of energy. We are experiencing the Big Freeze right here, as we called it back in the day. However, this time was pretty far off, as per my estimates. I was a cosmologist, after all. It seems very odd that this process happened too soon. It would happen much longer after my son, and I had long died," he explained.

Xanda found this bit new.

"Wait a minute. I thought you guys were immortal. Immortal means living forever. Is that not the case, or did I hear Emit wrong?" he asked.

Callahan laughed at that.

"Of course, we die. Who said we are immortal? It is just that our life spans are beyond your imagination. Emit probably said it to save himself some explaining. You see, so many races appear and disappear in one lifetime that we are immortal to others," he said, shrugging.

They stood in silence for a while.

Callahan continued again.

"So, basically, the universe from a trillion years from today will have expanded so much that no one would be able to see galaxies in the vicinity of the neighbourhood. Some of the galaxies will merge into others and stuff like that. This is not good because no new stars will form, which means no new life. Our existing life forms will continue to live and thrive, although thriving is relative. Our civilization would have easily thrived because we could manage that. I am unsure about primitive civilizations like yours that struggle with the basic stuff, let alone terraforming planets and starting anew. That would certainly be a difficulty for civilizations and planetary systems like yours. But then again, we were not expecting this to happen that quickly. It is like someone gamed the system or did something to trigger these events. That remains to be seen," he said.

At this moment, Emit emerged from inside. He was breathless and looked in agony at the two. He shrugged.

"I am confused. The last time I was here, I only saw the giant green star blowing away the solar system on its own. I was lucky enough to escape before it hit me. But then again, I do not recall the Big Freeze happening at the time. I have replayed the last memory a few times, but there was no freeze-death happening at the time. Someone is messing with the timeline of events and wants us dead badly. Who the hell could it be? Dad? Ideas?" he asked tersely.

Callahan shook his head.

"We did not have enemies, as per my recollection. It strikes odd to me as well. We were the good people, and taking us down would require sheer brilliance that only we were capable of. I do not think any other race or civilization equalled us in intelligence or weaponry," he said, dismissing the idea.

Emit was thinking about the possible culprit behind this.

Xanda spoke up.

"Hey! Sorry to interrupt, but how did we find your home planet so quickly? I remember waking up, and suddenly, I was staring at this huge ball of fire. Did you guys do something?" he asked nicely.

Emit was livid. Now was not the time for this question, though Callahan seemed forthcoming.

"Nothing happened. We accelerated the time-space continuum, so the *Infinite Corridor* ran faster than when you first saw it. Of course, you fell asleep and woke up much later. I think Emit has told you that time passes differently. That is the case inside that damned corridor as well. For us, it is more than only a minute or two. Different worlds passed by us that we saw. Some were too tempting, but we could not afford to go on side quests. I reckon we saw those theurgists on that planet. So, one can say they existed, but they were a scary bunch. I had a glimpse of them. Those creatures sure struck fear in my heart. Though we are immortal, they can kill us. Oh, and then we saw those barren planets that still have magic. The good thing about this corridor is that it shows different time periods of the world, so that is why it takes longer," he explained.

Xanda looked at him blankly.

"And you choose to come to this timeline of your planet. Would it not be better to come at a prior timeline to see this through?" he asked.

Emit nodded.

"I know, and I did think of that. We just got too excited when our planet came. Everything was forgotten at that moment until I realized my error in judgment. Anyhow, I think the *Infinite Corridor* changes events. It is not a perfect system and plays with timelines, which is annoying. I was not expecting this kind of imperfection that changes the entire universe. Or maybe someone else has played a hand. I am unsure of that. Worlds may merge into one another. At least we have come to the right place, but that is about it," he said.

"So, what do we do now? Escape from here back into that corridor?" he asked.

Emit seemingly had a plan.

"We stay right here and figure this out," he said.

"Although we should not forget that whoever this is could have used the disappearing library or this corridor to their advantage. Or have tools beyond your understanding. That is very much possible," he reflected on his journey thus far.

Emit's eyes lit up.

"I have an idea. But it is not going to be a pretty one," he said and disappeared without an explanation into his cockpit.

Callahan looked at his home planet in dismay. Maybe he would live again.

And then, all of a sudden, the sun disappeared from plain sight.

"Where did it go? Emit must have done something to it. Otherwise, how can something like that go away just like that?" Xanda shouted.

This was a good thing as well. The blue ice in the vicinity and far recesses of the solar system was melting, ebbing away.

"I think the ice is melting, which means things will return to normalcy. Whatever Emit has pulled off must be laudable. Our sun is gone for good. But no worries. We can always have a new sun in its place. Someone tampered with it and brought it to an early death," Callahan explained.

Suddenly, a bright light emerged from the sky. However, it disappeared as quickly as it had appeared.

Emit emerged from the corridor. His condition was dilapidated.

"You guys will not believe what happened? I came across those theurgists. That is a vicious bunch. They unleashed those humongous Androids, mighty energy hydras, and enormous monoliths animated via quantum micro-machines on me when they saw me. It was an army of them," he explained.

His dad seemed to know something.

"And you ripped them apart?" he asked.

Emit nodded.

Xanda was surprised that Emit (and even Callahan) could rip objects out of existence just by sheer thought.

"Yes, we can. We can do so much. You have no idea," Emit said.

He continued.

"So, they saw that these dark creatures were not something that threatened me, so they resorted to other tactics. I tried to rip them into shreds, but they were protected by powerful magic. They threw vicious spells at me, which I blocked with an ancient shield from their playbook. They looked surprised by that. However, I threw their dark creatures back at them, but it was a diversion. You see, they deflected those creatures while stepping back. Unwittingly, they stepped into the portal, and I closed it, much to their surprise," he said proudly.

Xanda seemed unimpressed.

"That does not solve anything, does it?" he said.

"Not exactly. The sun also went into this portal, and a bright light emerged, meaning the portal is destroyed, as are the theurgists and sun inside it," he boasted.

Xanda was left astounded.

"How did you do that?" he exclaimed in surprise.

He smiled at that.

"Well, let us just say it was a taste of their own medicine," he said, pivoting the spaceship towards Centaurus Prime.

Epilogue

It was tranquil on the western front. The spaceship with Callahan, Xanda and Emit landed on the space station of Centaurus Prime. Xanda looked around. It was the same as he had seen the planet in his dreams.

"Wow," he said as the air kissed his face.

The space station was in the middle of the jungle.

Some of the birds were walking with slender legs. Massive land animals had ferocious wings that flew over their heads. And the rain. That damned rain emerged from the ground, moving the sky upwards as he remembered.

"What the heck is this place? I mean, who the hell can survive here? Everything is counterintuitive here," he complained.

Callahan and Emit walked ahead, chuckling. The lad would catch on soon in time.

"I will have you back to normal once we reach the lab," Emit said.

Callahan nodded.

He stared at the screen.

"Wait a minute. This is weird. The dark matter is transitioning into the white matter. This can mean only one thing. The universe is reaching a state of equilibrium as all the dark matter will become white matter. The energy levels in the universe have averaged out," he noted.

Emit stepped on Centaurus Prime for the first time.

"God dammit," he realized.

He then remembered that everything was backward on Emit's planet. He took a few steps and began walking backwards. Wait. He had a brainwave. What if?

He took deep few breaths and jumped. To his surprise, he jumped forward this time, taking a massive leap as he did, leaving Emit and Callahan in shock. Xanda soared over the clouds until he landed back on the ground. There was something about this planet.

"Was that possible on our planet, dad?" he asked, turning to him.

Callahan shrugged.

"See! What I tell you! The child will find his way here eventually. And no, I never knew this was possible," he said casually.

Suddenly, the clouds cleared away, paving the way toward a greyish face.

There was a look of recognition on Emit's face.

"Do you know who that is?" Xanda asked.

"I am not sure. Seems familiar," he said, hiding a smile.

"Maximus," Callahan said.